TROUBLE AT THE BROWNSTONE

TROUBLE AT THE BROWNSTONE

A Nero Wolfe Mystery

Robert Goldsborough

MYSTERIOUSPRESS.COM

INTEGRATED MEDIA
NEW YORK

Author photo by Colleen Berg

978-1-5040-6662-4

Published in 2021 by MysteriousPress.com/Open Road Integrated Media, Inc.
180 Maiden Lane
New York, NY 10038
www.mysteriouspress.com
www.openroadmedia.com

To a quartet of good friends and fine people:

Tracy Oleksy and John Cline, who
champion the role of the independent bookstore
and
Authors Luisa Buehler and
Michael A. Black, for
consistent support and encouragement
of me and of other mystery writers

TROUBLE AT THE BROWNSTONE

CHAPTER 1

Let's get something straight, right at the start: I am not a friend of Theodore Horstmann's and never have been, from the first time we met in Nero Wolfe's brownstone all those years ago. He is surly, smug, standoffish, and superior in his manner. Oh, and honesty compels me to mention that Theodore doesn't like me, either, although you will have to ask him why. I'm not about to. And I don't care.

All of that aside, the man is part of our "family" in the old brownstone on West Thirty-Fifth Street in Manhattan, which consists of Nero Wolfe, master detective and lord of all he surveys; Fritz Brenner, chef supreme, whose gourmet meals are part of the reason Wolfe weighs a seventh of a ton; Horstmann, the orchid nurse who works with Wolfe to coddle the 10,000 orchids in the greenhouse's three climate-controlled rooms on the roof; and me, Archie Goodwin, gofer, errand boy, and cockle burr under Wolfe's saddle whenever he shows signs of laziness while working on a case—which is often. Life in the brownstone had gone smoothly since the end of the war, and now, six years later and just past the midpoint of the twentieth century, that domestic peace had been disturbed.

Because Theodore is part of our aforementioned family, any animosity I have for him gets set aside when he encounters trouble, which he did just last night, and in spades. Wolfe and I were in the dining room that June evening, feasting on Fritz's lamb cutlets and tomatoes, when the front bell began ringing with short, angry bursts, as if a telegrapher were exercising a finger. Fritz beat me to the hallway, but I was right behind him when—after peering through the one-way glass—he swung the front door open and a battered and bleeding Theodore Horstmann pitched forward into the hallway with a groan, falling down on the floor, writhing.

"There were . . . two of them . . ." he gasped, looking at Fritz and me through blackened eyes that were barely open. By now, Wolfe had joined us and peered down at Theodore, his eyebrows going halfway up his forehead. "Great hounds and Cerberus!" Wolfe barked. "Get Dr. Vollmer—now!"

Doc Vollmer, Edwin A., to be formal, is our local sawbones and lives just down the block. He has been both a friend to Wolfe and a confidant who has patched me up on occasion. Vollmer also has, when necessary, hidden one of our clients in his house and once signed a certificate that stated Wolfe was batty.

Less than five minutes after I called him, Vollmer, a short specimen with large eyes, a round face, and not much chin, barreled in with his bag and looked down at Theodore, to whom Fritz, on the floor, was ministering with a cup of water and a cool compress on his forehead.

"Get out of my way!" Vollmer said, his sharp tongue belying his stature, as he knelt beside Theodore and began checking his vital signs—pulse, carotid, blood pressure. He spoke to the wounded man but got no answer, as he had lapsed into labored breathing. "Archie, call an ambulance," he spat over his shoulder. "We are going to Roosevelt Hospital—now!"

I followed orders, and within minutes, accompanied by the sound of a siren and screeching brakes, a pair of young, square-jawed men in white coats burst into the hall with a stretcher and eased Theodore onto it as Vollmer barked orders at them with all the authority of a drill sergeant. "I will call you when I know something," the doctor said over his shoulder to Wolfe as he and the trio, one of them clearly unconscious, left the brownstone.

For one of the few times I have known him, Wolfe was both speechless and unmoored. It was enough that his dinner had been interrupted, an almost unthinkable occurrence, but his comfortable and insular world suddenly got turned upside down. Theodore had worked for Wolfe for decades, and while it's true the two of them often sparred—sometimes noisily— over the proper care of one variety of orchid or another, Wolfe had come to rely upon this brusque and often surly man—probably more than he would admit.

A few months back, Theodore had vacated his small quarters on the roof that adjoined the rooms in which those pampered posies reside and flourish. He told Wolfe he felt the need to have a place of his own, that he felt closed-in by spending all of his waking and sleeping hours inside the brownstone. Wolfe couldn't argue the point, nor did he try, despite his own reluctance to leave home except for the occasional foray to the barbershop or his annual visit to the Metropolitan Orchid Show, where he was always seen as something of a celebrity.

Theodore had moved into a one-bedroom apartment in a five-story building called the Elmont on Tenth Avenue, just north of Fifty-Eighth, a brisk walk from the brownstone. He still continued to eat both breakfast and lunch in the kitchen with Fritz, and also ate dinner with him on many occasions. And, of course, he still spent those inviolable four hours a day—nine-to-eleven in the morning and four-to-six in the evening—with Wolfe up in the plant rooms. With the exception of Theodore's move to separate living quarters, life had seemed to continue apace on West Thirty-Fifth Street until that night he staggered up to the front door and collapsed.

Since then, he has remained in a coma, with Doc Vollmer telling us that "there is no telling when, or if, he will regain consciousness. Specialists agree with me on that assessment." Vollmer had Theodore moved to intensive care at the hospital, and after a weekday lunch, Wolfe had me drive him there to see the patient. We walked along the facility's halls with a white-jacketed resident who had the requisite stethoscope draped around his neck. He seemed impressed by meeting Nero Wolfe.

"I hope that you will not be shocked by Mr. Horstmann's appearance," the young doctor told us earnestly as we stopped at a room that had *T. Horstmann* typed on a card that fitted into a slot on the door. Grim-faced, Wolfe made no reply.

If he indeed was shocked at what he saw, he gave no indication as he stared down at the figure in the bed, who was surrounded by wires and tubes and with bandages covering much of his still-bruised face. After no more than a minute, Wolfe said, "Let us go."

As I steered the Heron back to West Thirty-Fifth Street with my passenger in the back seat clutching the specially installed hand strap as if it were a lifeline, he said, "We will find whoever did this. Do you question that?"

"No, sir, not for a moment," I replied, wondering how much of the plural pronoun would fall to me to accomplish. But that did not matter; this was in the family.

After we got home from the hospital, Wolfe settled into the reinforced chair at his desk, grimaced, and snapped, "Get Fritz."

I took that as a command and went to the kitchen, where Brenner was preparing one of tomorrow's meals. "Mr. Wolfe would like to see you," I told him.

He looked confused. "Does he want beer?"

"No, he wants you—now."

He put down his oven mitts and spatula and followed me into the office, his face lined with concern.

"Yes, sir," he said to Wolfe, standing at attention.

"Sit down, Fritz. You have the advantage of me."

"Sir?" He clearly was uncomfortable. To him, the office was not a place where he belonged, other than to bring beer when requested and to run the vacuum cleaner and do the dusting, but only when no one else was present.

Fritz looked at me in confusion and finally chose one of the yellow chairs that faced Wolfe's desk. He was not about to park himself in the red leather chair that was reserved for clients or for Inspector Cramer of the Homicide Squad.

"You know more about Theodore and his private life than either Archie or I do," Wolfe said. "I would—"

"How is he, Mr. Wolfe?" he interrupted.

"I should have started with that, Fritz; my apologies. Theodore is comatose, but his condition appears to be stable. As to when he may emerge from the coma, that remains uncertain. We would like to learn what you know about his life away from here. All of my conversations with him have invariably been about orchids. And as you are no doubt aware, Archie has not had any substantive conversations whatever with him."

Fritz licked his lips and frowned. "I do not know what I can say to you."

"Very well," Wolfe said. "I will assume the role of interrogator. What can you tell us about Theodore's place of residence?"

"I have not been there, but from what he has told me, he finds it to be comfortable. It has one bedroom, he says, and it is on the fourth floor of an apartment building on Tenth Avenue up in the Fifties. He can walk down here in less than a half hour."

"We have the address, of course," Wolfe said, "so any mail that comes to us is forwarded. Has he said anything to you about his activities away from the brownstone?"

Fritz nodded. "Oh yes, he tells me he has found a new hobby—bridge."

"Indeed."

"Actually, he told me he had learned to play years ago, but only since he moved had he started to take up the game again. He seems to enjoy it, and he said he plays two or three nights a week."

"With whom does the play? And where?"

"Other men of about his age. He told me they are divorced or have never married. They have their games in a back room of a bar on Tenth Avenue, which is called McCready's. It is just across the street from where he now lives."

Wolfe threw a questioning look in my direction. "I know of the saloon," I said. "It's a fixture in that neighborhood, and it's been there as long as I can remember. I stopped in once a while back because of a case we were working on, although the lead I was chasing turned out to be a dead end. Because it is not far from the North River piers on the Hudson, it's a hangout for a lot of longshoremen."

"That's right," Fritz put it. "Theodore told me that dockworkers like the place, both for drinking and for playing pocket billiards—or pool, as it is called. He also said that they seemed to be a pretty rough bunch. And they shoot pool in the same room where the bridge games are."

"Longshoremen can be tough, all right," I agreed. "Seems like an odd combination of customers that McCready's draws—dockworkers and middle-aged card players."

Fritz continued to look uncomfortable, which was not lost on Wolfe. "Is there anything else you can tell us about Theodore?"

"Only that he asked his bridge-playing friends, and he referred to them as friends, to call him 'Ted.'"

"Did he tell you if any of those men knew what he does for a living?" I posed.

"I did ask him that, Archie, but he said he only told them he worked as a gardener."

"Didn't they think it strange that somebody living in the middle of Manhattan would be a gardener?"

"I guess they would," Fritz said with a shrug, "although Theodore never mentioned their reactions to me."

"Did he ever suggest anyone in that bar who might have had animus toward him?" Wolfe asked.

"No, sir. I got the impression Theodore thought the dockworkers were rather crude and that they felt the card players were not overly . . . I don't know how to express it."

"Manly?" Wolfe supplied.

"Yes, that is it, manly. But according to Theodore, he and his new friends ignored the others in the bar and those around the pocket billiard table in the back room."

"Being ignored probably bothered the dockworkers," I put in.

"No doubt," Wolfe concurred. "Nothing riles the swaggerer more than to be disregarded. Thank you, Fritz; we will take no more of your time."

What Wolfe really was saying was that it was necessary for

Fritz to get back to his meal preparations. We were faced with an upsetting and potentially tragic situation, but that did not mean the meticulous schedule by which the brownstone operated was about to go out the window.

CHAPTER 2

The next morning just after eleven, Wolfe came down from his two-hour session with the orchids up on the roof, got settled behind his desk, rang for beer, and said to me, "Get Mr. Hewitt on the telephone."

For those of you who are new to these narratives, Lewis Hewitt is a wealthy man-about-town and also an orchid fancier whose collection rivals Wolfe's. The two have engaged in an essentially civil but spirited competition over the years and dine at each other's home once a year. I dialed the number of Hewitt's estate on Long Island and got a frosty, British-sounding male voice that informed me I had reached "the Hewitt residence."

"Lewis Hewitt, please, Nero Wolfe is calling."

"Just one moment, please," Frosty sniffed as I nodded to Wolfe to pick up his instrument. I stayed on the line, which is standard procedure unless I am told otherwise.

"Ah, Mr. Wolfe, it is so nice to hear from you," said the baritone Lewis Hewitt. "To what do I owe the pleasure?"

"Theodore Horstmann is indisposed at present, a condition likely to continue. I am seeking a replacement for the foreseeable future."

"Oh, dear, I do hope his situation is not serious."

"As do I, sir. But for now, I need an assistant in the plant rooms, one whom, if not as skilled as Mr. Horstmann, is competent to work with me on a regular basis, at least four hours a day."

"Of course. Off hand, I can think of two or maybe three possibilities. Would you care to interview them or have me send you their references?"

"I would prefer to meet each of them, unless you have a candidate you see as clearly superior to the others."

"Actually, I do," Hewitt said. "It is a man about Mr. Horstmann's age named Carl Willis. He has served well as an adequate replacement when my regular gardener was on vacation, and he also has worked on occasion for several of my neighbors out here on the island. They all have told me they found him satisfactory and would be happy to have him fill in for them again when the need arises."

"Does he have some form of regular employment?"

"Yes and no," Hewitt replied. "That is, he works part-time at a large garden center near where I live, but his hours there are extremely flexible, and the center is happy to have him whenever he is available. Would you like to meet him?"

"I would," Wolfe said. "Please have him call Mr. Goodwin to set up an appointment. Three o'clock would be an ideal time." Hewitt said he would follow through, and the call was ended.

I swiveled to face Wolfe and started to say something when the doorbell rang. I went down the hall and saw a thick and familiar silhouette through the one-way glass. "Well, it has been a long time," I said to Inspector Lionel T. Cramer, head of the Homicide Squad. "Have you been avoiding us?"

"As much as possible," Cramer growled. "Wolfe should be down from playing with his posies, right?" Before I could respond, he barreled down the hall to the office and made a bee-line to his usual landing place, the red leather chair.

Wolfe considered him with raised eyebrows. "Mr. Cramer?"

"Don't tell me you're wondering why I'm here," the burly cop said, pulling a cigar out of his pocket and jamming it unlit into his mouth.

"We don't have any cases at the moment that would interest you," Wolfe said.

"Yeah? Where's your orchid guy, what's his name . . . Horstmann?"

"Why do you ask?"

"I ask because, goddammit, I happen to know where he is—in intensive care at Roosevelt Hospital."

"You have answered your own question, sir."

"You don't deny it?"

"I do not."

"I understand Horstmann got beat up, and pretty badly. How is it that you never got in touch with us about this?"

"Unless there has been a departmental restructuring I have not been made aware of, you are in charge of investigating homicides in New York, and there has been no homicide involving Mr. Horstmann."

"We also happen to investigate *attempted* homicides," Cramer said, "and from what I have learned about Horstmann's condition and the circumstances for his admission to the hospital, someone tried very hard to make him a homicide the other day."

"You seem to have good sources, which should not surprise me," Wolfe remarked.

Cramer gnawed on his stogie and leaned forward, jabbing a beefy index finger at Wolfe. "Look, whenever anyone gets brought into a hospital in this town—whether by ambulance, family, friend, or doctor—and has been shot or beaten the way we've learned Horstmann was—we hear about it. Now I know you would be the first to tell me that I am not Einstein, but when I hear the name Theodore Horstmann, I am smart enough to remember that he works for you. And when someone who works for you is in trouble, I get suspicious. It's probably an occupational hazard."

"Probably," Wolfe replied.

"What I don't understand—or maybe I do—is why you failed to mention what happened to Horstmann to the police. Could it be that you want to solve this mystery yourself, without outside help? Or maybe this isn't a mystery at all to you."

Wolfe set down his beer glass and dabbed his lips with a handkerchief. "Mr. Cramer, I am at a loss as to what befell Theodore. I saw no reason to bring you into what may well be an aborted robbery attempt."

"You say *aborted*. Did Horstmann have any money on him when, as I understand, he came here before he collapsed?"

"He did," Wolfe said. "Not a lot of cash, but enough that someone would have taken it had they not been distracted, perhaps by a passerby."

"Now you're just speculating," Cramer snapped. "Did Horstmann tell you anything when he got here?"

"Just the words 'There were two of them.' That is all he managed to get out before lapsing into unconsciousness."

"I take it you have his wallet."

"We do," Wolfe said. "We were not about to leave it with him when he was taken to the hospital. Dr. Vollmer went along to identify him to the staff."

"Somehow, I don't think you are leveling with me, Wolfe," the inspector said, rolling the unlit cigar around in his mouth. "Maybe it's because of our past history that makes me suspicious."

"Suspicious of what, sir?" Wolfe asked, flipping a palm.

"I don't know. But you do not seem terribly interested in any help from us in finding out what happened to a man who has been in your employ for Lord knows how many years."

"I assure you I have no hidden reason to eschew your aid. I feel we, Mr. Goodwin and I, can handle this ourselves. And we mean no disrespect."

"Suit yourself," Cramer said, shaking his head. "I've got enough on my plate that I don't need anything else. But somehow, I feel as though I haven't heard the last of this." With that, he put the gnawed cigar back in his breast pocket, stood up, and stormed out. I followed him down the hall at a respectful distance and locked the front door as he walked down the steps and climbed into an unmarked black Ford sedan.

"Well, at least he didn't fling his damned el ropo at the wastebasket today," I said. "With his lousy aim, it always ends up on the floor for me to pitch."

Wolfe scowled and said nothing, closing his eyes and leaning back in his reinforced chair. After a minute, I broke the silence. "You've always told me the police have one great advantage over us: manpower. While we have me, Saul Panzer, Fred Durkin, and Orrie Cather, they have an army. I am wondering why we don't take advantage of that army and let them delve into what happened to Theodore."

"Archie, do you deny the police would make a hash of it?"

"Maybe they would," I conceded. "Well, yeah . . . probably. But we're capable of making a hash of it as well."

"Perhaps. However, I happen to like our chances. As I understand, you are a good bridge player."

"I don't recall ever telling you that."

"You didn't, but Miss Rowan did."

A pause here to introduce Lily Rowan. She is a very good friend and has been for years, ever since she saw me outrun an angry bull in an upstate pasture and then leap over a fence to avoid its horns.* From that day forth, she has called me "Escamillo," after a toreador in the opera *Carmen*. As to the specifics of our relationship, that is nobody's business but our own.

"I never knew that Lily mentioned my bridge playing to you."

The creases in Wolfe's cheeks deepened, his version of a smile. "Once some years ago, she was up in the plant rooms admiring orchids when she happened to mention the two of you would be playing bridge that night. 'Is Archie skilled at the game?' I asked, and Miss Rowan quickly replied, 'Oh yes, he has a killer instinct. I always want him as a partner, because I know our chances of winning are extremely good.'"

"I should probably blush. I think I know where you're going with this."

"I am sure you do. It is highly possible the bridge game Theodore was part of is currently in need of a fourth participant."

"That is where I thought you were going. All right, so you want me to show up at McCready's and figure out how I can worm my way into that backroom bridge game."

"Precisely."

"And what if they have already found themselves a new player to replace Theodore?"

---

* From *Some Buried Caesar* by Rex Stout (1939)

Wolfe drew in a bushel of air and exhaled slowly. "Archie, I have full confidence in your resourcefulness."

"Thanks a whole heap. I'm guessing that, assuming I do get into the game, you want me gauge the skills of the others at the table and play to their level. The last thing I need is to be seen as a bridge hustler."

"You have answered a principal concern. Did you learn from Fritz on which nights Theodore played at McCready's?"

"No, but I will."

"Also, I think a visit to Theodore's apartment also is called for. When his pockets were emptied the other night, keys were among the items Fritz retrieved."

"Which do you want me to do first, search the apartment or worm myself into the bridge game?"

"Act in the light of experience as guided by intelligence."

That is one of Wolfe's ways of saying, "You're on your own."

CHAPTER 3

The next morning, I was starting breakfast at my small table in the kitchen as usual and reading my copy of the *New York Times* when Fritz said, "Mr. Wolfe asked me to give you this when I served him up in his room." He handed me a folded slip of paper that I opened, seeing the writing in Wolfe's neat hand.

> AG
>> Carl Willis has a 9:30 a.m. appointment with me. Kindly bring him up to the plant rooms.
> NW

"So, Theodore's temporary replacement will be coming this morning," I said, showing Fritz the note. "Of course, that is contingent upon Mr. Wolfe's approval," I added.

"Is there any change in Theodore's condition?"

"Doc Vollmer probably will call this morning with an update, as he has been doing on a daily basis," I told Fritz. "I will let you know what we hear. Or you may be the one to answer the phone and get the information."

After my breakfast of wheat cakes, sausage, orange juice, and blueberry muffins, I sat with coffee in the office, opening the morning mail and paying a handful of bills. At nine thirty sharp, the doorbell rang and I went down the hall, seeing a slender figure through the glass.

When I swung open the door, I found myself facing a short and wiry man of about sixty-five who blinked and looked at me with an expression of uncertainty.

"Is this the residence of Mr. Nero Wolfe?" he asked, taking off his flat cap and kneading it with nervous hands.

"It is indeed," I told him. "And you are Mr. Willis, I presume?"

"Yes, sir," he said, swallowing hard and continuing to twist the cap.

I introduced myself and ushered him in. "Mr. Wolfe is expecting you, and I'll lead the way." He followed me down the hall, and we stepped into the elevator.

"Mr. Wolfe uses this several times a day," I told Willis as we rumbled upward in the moving closet. Our visitor remained tense, which made me wonder if Lewis Hewitt had painted Wolfe as a stern taskmaster. If so, it's probably just as well, I thought; better that than be surprised at the brusqueness and lack of warmth of his potential employer.

When we got to the top of the brownstone and into the plant rooms, we found Wolfe at one of the benches, wearing an apron and glaring down at a purple *cattleya* as if it had somehow disappointed him. We stood in the doorway and I cleared my throat, causing Wolfe to look up and glare in my direction.

"Mr. Willis, meet Nero Wolfe," I said, stepping back and saying to my boss, "This is Carl Willis." Our visitor stepped forward shyly and held out a paw, which Wolfe—who hates shaking hands—reluctantly took, having no alternative. If Willis was taken aback by Wolfe's girth, he didn't show it, but then he likely had been prepped by Hewitt about this as well as Wolfe's temperament.

Wolfe glared at me again, my cue to leave. As I walked out and started down the stairway, I heard Wolfe say, "And this is the way I expect you to . . ."

Back in the office, I got the keys to Theodore's apartment, which I had kept in my top desk drawer since we took them from his pocket. The walk north up Tenth Avenue took me about twenty minutes. His building, like many others around it, was five stories, with shops at street level that included a barbershop, a dry cleaner, and a deli. Next to the lobby entrance was a faded brass plaque that read *The Elmont*. If giving the place a name that was meant to confer class, it failed.

The small, unadorned lobby, wedged between two of the business establishments at street level, had a self-service elevator but no doorman or hall man. The Elmont was that sort of place. I rode up alone and went along a dimly lit corridor to 412, fitting the key into the lock and pushing the door open.

The living room was compact and neat, with two curtained windows looking out onto the bustle of Tenth Avenue. The furnishings consisted of a sofa with a plaid slipcover, two stuffed chairs, an end table with a lamp, one floor lamp, and a small bookcase. There was no television set or radio.

I looked at Theodore's books. Three, as could be expected, were about orchids, others were *The World Almanac* and a dictionary, and, befitting the man's new hobby, *Contract Bridge in a Nutshell,* by Charles Goren. I rifled through each of the books, but nothing fell out. The only other items on the shelves were copies of recent gardening and news magazines, which I also shook, without success.

The drawer in the end table was empty save for a set of plastic coasters and a deck of well-used cards. Perhaps he practiced dealing bridge hands to sharpen his bidding and playing skills.

The bedroom with a neatly made bed proclaimed an overall tidiness, hardly surprising, given that Theodore had always kept his small living area in the brownstone in good order. I rooted through his chest of drawers, finding nothing more than what might be expected: neatly folded shirts, underwear, socks, and two pairs of pajamas. The closet also held no surprises: Slacks, six pairs of them, on hangers, along with one tweed sports coat, three neckties on pegs, two zippered windbreakers, a flat cap, and an overcoat.

An electric alarm clock sat atop the bedside table, which contained two drawers, both of which were empty. Nothing of interest was to be found either in the bathroom, with its almost empty medicine cabinet, or the narrow pullman kitchen. Theodore clearly did not prepare his own meals. After all, he still had breakfast and lunch in the brownstone kitchen with Fritz, and on occasion, dinner as well. He did, however, make coffee for himself, as the stained pot on the counter suggested.

In all, this was a place that had only the slightest of lived-in looks, which made it difficult to imagine that its tenant did much more than sleep here. I made one more pass through the unit and left, planning to visit McCready's Bar that night.

I got back to the brownstone just before Wolfe came down from the plant rooms. "Well, how is Mr. Willis working out?" I asked as he lowered himself into his chair, placing a raceme of orange *laelia* in the small vase on his desk and ringing for beer.

"He appears to be adequate, nothing more."

"Does that mean that you will keep him on?"

Wolfe raised his shoulders slightly and let them down in his version of a shrug. "I feel I have little choice, especially as Mr. Hewitt seems to feel this man is the best of those he said were available."

"Try not to be too hard on him," I counseled—as if he would ever be likely to take my counsel. "After all, it took you a long time to break Theodore in, as I recall."

My answer was a scowl, as is often the reaction I get from Wolfe when I have scored a point in a discussion.

CHAPTER 4

After a dinner of veal birds in casserole with mushrooms and white wine, followed by raspberries in sherry cream, I chose to forgo coffee in the office with Wolfe and walked out into the night instead, my destination: McCready's Bar on Tenth Avenue.

From the outside, the saloon looked like countless other Manhattan watering holes, Irish or otherwise. A pair of bright neon signs cut the night gloom, advertising competing beers, along with a hand-lettered poster that read HAPPY HOUR WITH FREE SNAX and was surrounded by decals of shamrocks.

I pushed inside to the sound of a jukebox playing Sinatra. Faces, all male, at the long bar that ran along the left side of the room, turned in unison to consider me and then quickly swiveled back to their drinks, mostly beer, and focused on the Yankee game on the TV set. I went to the far end of the bar and, although I have never been big on beer, I ordered a draft from a lanky young bartender.

"I heard there's a card game in here," I asked as he slid a foamy stein in my direction.

"Ah, but if you are looking for big-time gambling, this surely is not the place you would be wanting," the bartender said. "Those gents in the back room, they indulge in games like pinochle and bridge. Not much coinage changes hands, which is jake with the boss. And they buy enough drinks to keep him happy."

"I play those games, too," I told him.

"Well, then you might be just the very fellow that they are looking for," he said, jabbing a thumb toward a partly open door in the back.

The smoky room turned out to be surprisingly large, compared to the cramped quarters of the barroom. At the back, four men slouched around a pool table, cues in hand and cigarettes dangling from lips. They could have served as models for a John Sloan painting, circa 1925. Much closer to me, three men somewhere between fifty-five and seventy clutched cards in their hands as they leaned forward across table from one another.

I stood watching silently until one of them, wearing half-glasses and a wary expression, turned toward me, his face a question mark.

Before he could speak, I asked, "What're you playing?"

"Pinochle," he said without enthusiasm.

"Good game for three," I replied.

"Yeah, but for us, it's not anywhere near as much fun as bridge. Say, do you play bridge, by any chance?"

"I do, although I'm no Goren or Jacoby or Blackwood."

"Since you even know those names, you should fit in here. Want to play a few hands?"

"Before you sit down," a second man, with wisps of hair and

needing to go on a diet, cautioned, "in all honesty, we aren't that great, but we do have a good time. And unlike those hotshots who play in big tournaments, we don't go getting mad at each other. And we don't use a lot of those fancy bidding systems. It's straight rubber bridge, right out of good old Charlie Goren, none of this duplicate stuff and none of those goofy bids that have become popular."

"That sounds good to me," I said. "By the way, I'm Art."

"And I'm Sid," said the one with the goatee, shaking my hand. "This is Harvey," he went on, motioning to the guy with the half-glasses and a squint. "And over there is Chester," he said, indicating the one who was overweight. "He's the one who got us together after we met at some YMCA bridge lessons." Chester, who could give Nero Wolfe competition in the weight category, smiled and nodded, which made his jowls jiggle like Jell-O.

"All right, Art, have yourself a chair and we'll draw for partners—high and low card are a team." Sid and I ended up against Harvey and Chester. All three them of them turned out to be fairly good, and I played at their level, even if it meant dropping my game down a notch.

After two hands, with each team having made its bid, I asked, "Who is usually your fourth?"

"A very nice fellow named Ted," Chester replied. "He had played with us for, oh . . . a couple of months or more, it's been. But he just quit coming a week or so back, and we don't know why. He never mentioned where he lived, so we have no way of getting ahold of him. We just hope he isn't sick or something."

"What is this Ted like?"

"As I said, he is very nice, polite, and very much on the quiet side," Chester said. "Told us that he hadn't been playing bridge for all that long, but he seemed to know what he was doing. And he sure enjoyed himself."

"I wonder if he's retired," I said.

Sid laughed. "You mean like us? We all are pensioners. I was a barber, Chester here worked at the post office, and Harvey sold insurance. But it sounded like Ted was still getting a paycheck; he said he worked as some kind of gardener. You still working, Art? You look like you're young enough."

I had planned to say I was an insurance investigator if asked, but when Harvey turned out to have worked in the insurance business, I figured he would ask questions about my employer and find me out as a fraud, so I switched horses: "I'm at a small company that does job printing for actuarial companies—all kinds of brochures and folders full of tables about life expectancy, stuff like that." That had the desired effect—a total lack of interest among my audience.

"You married, Art?" Harvey asked.

"Nope, I guess nobody would have me," I replied with a self-deprecating chuckle.

"None of us are married, either," Sid replied, "although I was once, but we both decided we weren't suited for each other. And we were both right."

"Me, I never even gave it a shot," Chester put in with a small laugh that was enough to get those jowls jiggling again. Harvey shrugged, saying of marriage, "no one ever came along who made me want to give up the life I was leading."

"Yeah, when you're a playboy, you hate to get tied down," Sid said to a chorus of laughter.

"Some playboy," Harvey replied. "Once I went two years without a date. But I wasn't complaining. I could do what I wanted to and *when* I wanted to."

The others clapped, and Sid said, turning to Chester, "Enough talking, Miller. Let's deal 'em out."

The rest of the evening was uneventful, other than occasional swearing and raucous laughter from the nearby pool players. "They can be a pain," Sid observed quietly, "and they don't much like us—we're just too lame for a bunch of longshoremen. Ted really seemed to dislike them—as well as the other dockworkers who fill up the bar most nights—even more than the rest of us did. He once said they were 'up to no good.'"

"Hmm, interesting. Did he get specific?"

"No, and he acted kind of mysterious when we asked him about that. But when we were playing, I did notice that he seemed to have one ear cocked to the conversation around the pool table."

"Did you hear anything from those guys that made you suspicious?"

"I didn't," Sid said. "How about you two?"

Both Chester and Harvey shook their heads. "I've mainly heard them cursing and talking about women—and not very respectfully," Harvey said. We were far enough away from the pool table that we couldn't be heard by the guys with the cue sticks.

"It isn't always the same bunch who shoot pool," Chester said, "but as far as I'm concerned, they're interchangeable, and they are all rough around the edges. And some of them behave like they're hiding something, although damned if I know what that is. It does make you curious, though."

As if on cue, so to speak, one of the pool players, a chunky character with tattoos on both of his thick arms, walked by our table, probably on his way to the bar. He sneered and said, "Having fun in your little game, boys?" Chester started to answer, then decided discretion was the better part of valor and clammed up, biting his lower lip.

I wanted to ask more about Theodore but didn't want to appear too nosy, so I shifted gears. "Turns out we were more or less even tonight," I said, looking at the score pad, which Sid kept. "One rubber each, although you two"—I nodded to Chester and Harvey—"finished with two hundred more points than us. Congratulations."

"Hope you can join us again," Harvey said, "if we don't get Ted back. We're usually here Tuesday, Wednesday, and Thursday nights—Fridays there's just too much noise in the bar. If there are only three of us, we play pinochle as we were doing when you came. But bridge is more fun, at least as far as we're concerned."

I told them I agreed about bridge and said that they might see me again. When I got back home, Wolfe was still at his desk, rereading *The Oregon Trail*, by Francis Parkman, a volume I had seen on the bookshelves since my earliest days in the brownstone. He looked up, eyes wide, suggesting that I report.

I gave him my impressions of the bar, the bridge group, and the longshoremen as he leaned back, eyes closed. "Theodore seems to be well-liked by the bridge players," I said as I provided Wolfe with a verbatim report on my conversations with Sid, Chester, and Harvey. "He apparently didn't tell them very much about himself, other than that he worked as a gardener. From what they told me, he didn't say where he was employed or give any specifics about his job."

"While you were away, I received a call from Theodore's sister, who as you know lives in New Jersey," Wolfe said. "She has been visiting him every day, and she told me he shows no indication of emerging from the coma."

"Not a good sign."

"However, Dr. Vollmer says he has known of numerous examples in which individuals regain consciousness and also their full faculties after long extended periods—sometimes months—in a comatose state."

"So, where do we go from here?"

Wolfe glared at his empty beer stein as if looking to it for inspiration. "Have Saul, Fred, and Orrie here tomorrow night at nine."

My employer thinks all he has to do is issue an order, and I will carry it out—the faster, the better. As I have said about Wolfe more than once, he never puts off until tomorrow what I can do today.

CHAPTER 5

In this case, it really was later the next day before I could fulfill Wolfe's order. I tried all three of our regular freelance operatives in the morning, but I struck out in each case. Two of them, Saul and Orrie, didn't answer their phones, and Fred's wife told me he was out tailing someone.

But I had total success in the afternoon, and by 9 p.m. they all were seated in the office. Saul Panzer, all five-feet-seven, 140 pounds, was perched in the red leather chair at the end of Wolfe's desk, befitting his status as the best human bloodhound on this side of the Atlantic Ocean. As usual, his mug, which is two-thirds nose, needed a shave, and also as usual, he came in wearing a battered flat cap and a sports coat that looked like it came off the rack at a secondhand shop.

In the yellow chairs facing Wolfe's desk sat Fred Durkin and Orrie Cather. Fred, thick in the middle and thin on top, may not be as savvy as Saul, but he is dogged, loyal, and tough. And he is second only to Saul in his ability to hold a tail. I once asked him the secret to his surveillance skill, and he deadpanned, "I just go up to the subject and ask him where he's headed, and then if I lose him, I know where to look." I suppose he knew how funny that was, but with Fred, I never can be sure.

Orrie, tall, handsome, and aware of it, thinks he's suave and in fact he has a good deal of success with the ladies—at least to hear him tell it. He also feels that he would be better at my job than I am, but he is not about to find out as long as I am upright and above ground. He is a good operative, but Saul and Fred happen to be better.

I refreshed our guests' drinks—scotch for Saul and Orrie and beer for Fred, as Wolfe—fresh from a conversation in the kitchen with Fritz about tomorrow's meals—walked into the office, nodded to each of the trio and thanked them for coming. He did not bother to thank me for rounding them up.

"Are any of you aware of Theodore's situation?" Wolfe asked as Fritz entered with his and Fred's beer. They all shook their heads, and their expressions indicated various degrees of puzzlement.

"As each of you may know, Theodore moved out of the brownstone some weeks ago and took an apartment in a building on Tenth Avenue, although he has continued to work for me on a regular schedule. On one night several days ago, he appeared at the door here in a state of collapse, having been savagely beaten. His only words before he lapsed into unconsciousness were, 'There were two of them.'"

"I'd like to get my hands on the sons-of-bitches who did that!" Cather barked, rising halfway out of his chair.

"As would we all, Orrie," Wolfe said, holding up a palm. "That is the purpose of this meeting." He then proceeded to summarize all that had transpired regarding Theodore and his participation in the bridge games at McCready's, as well as my report.

"Sounds like it was a simple mugging," Fred put in.

"So one might be tempted to think," Wolfe replied, "except that Theodore's billfold was in his pocket, containing thirty-five dollars, and his watch, of which he was very proud, remained on his wrist. It is possible, however, that his assailants were scared off by a pedestrian or a passing automobile."

"Who could have it in for Horstmann?" Saul posed. "I can't say I know him very well, but he hardly seems like the sort to make enemies."

"I believe we all can agree upon that, Saul," Wolfe said. "But it seems highly possible that Theodore was singled out for the beating. Robbery does not appear to be the intent."

Saul turned to me. "According to what one of those card players told you, Horstmann thought some of the longshoremen in the joint were 'up to no good,' right?"

"Yes, but that's as much as he said. It's not a lot to go on."

"Dockworkers can be a pretty rough bunch, but as far as I know, and I get around quite a lot," Saul said, "nothing questionable has been going on along the North River piers lately, and that's where the guys who hang out in McCready's would be working. After all, the bar's just a short walk from the Hudson."

Wolfe set his beer down and interlaced his hands over his middle mound. "Saul, you play bridge, don't you?'

"Yeah, but as much as it pains me to say this, Archie is better—not at poker or gin rummy, mind you—but at bridge. It's no contest."

"I trust you to be adequate, however," Wolfe said. "Those gentlemen who play at McCready's know Archie now, and it would be difficult for him to extract any further information from them about Theodore without appearing overly inquisitive. You, however, can start with a clean slate by insinuating yourself into their game. Perhaps you will be able to learn more about Theodore's behavior and his apparent suspicions about the customers in this public house. Tomorrow is Thursday, which means the threesome will presumably be seeking a fourth for a bridge game."

"I will give it a shot," Saul said.

Wolfe turned to Fred. "I would like you to sit at the bar in McCready's tomorrow and absorb as much information as you can about the place. Do you feel you will be able to blend in?"

Fred grinned. "Like Saul says, I will give it a shot. I have never been paid to go drinking before."

"Don't get carried away with the assignment," Wolfe said dryly, "and do not acknowledge Saul's presence. Orrie, you will go to the residential building where Theodore has been living and find out anything you can about him from his neighbors. You can tell them he has disappeared and that you are a friend seeking information about his possible whereabouts. It is possible, although not likely, given Theodore's taciturn nature, that he may have shared suspicions he had about people in McCready's."

"Sure, I can be a cousin or something like that," Orrie said. "Do you want me to go through Theodore's apartment, too?"

"Archie already has searched it, so there is no need for that at present. You should also make inquiries at establishments in that neighborhood—cleaners, restaurants, drugstores—to learn anything you can about his recent behavior."

"I really should have a picture of him," Orrie said.

"Of course. Archie, I believe we have photographs of Theodore in his file."

"We do. I'll pull one out," I said.

"I remind each of you that Theodore has been calling himself

'Ted', at least to the card players," Wolfe said. "That may well be the name he's known by to anyone you talk to."

"What's Archie going to do?" Orrie asked. He has always been unduly interested in my roles in cases, probably thinking he could do a better job on any particular assignment than me.

"He will conduct reconnaissance on the Hudson River docks, an area he has some familiarity with." Wolfe was referring, at least in part, to my first job on coming to New York, when I was hired as an armed guard to patrol one company's docks because of concerns of thefts from ships moored there.

"Very well, gentlemen," Wolfe said, "we will convene tomorrow night at nine and review your experiences. I caution you all to avoid mentioning the attack on Theodore. Act as if each of you is puzzled as to why he has disappeared."

When Wolfe referenced my work as a guard on the docks, he was diplomatic enough not to bring up what an inauspicious start it was for me in New York. On patrol one night, I had spotted two thieves trying to board one of the ships. They shot at me and I returned fire, killing them both. I wasn't charged, but I got fired from my job anyway.*

An upshot of that unfortunate experience on the Hudson pier was that I got to know a guy who had run a docking operation for years. In a case we worked on, where we found that whole shipments of Swiss watches and expensive clocks were disappearing, I met Charlie King of Cabot & Sons Importers, who managed the company's crews on their pier. With the help of Saul Panzer's savvy and Wolfe's brain, we nailed two of the company's sticky-fingered longshoremen, and King has been grateful ever since, as his own job had been on the line until those bad apples got smoked out.

---

* From *Fourth of July Picnic* in the book *And Four to Go* by Rex Stout (1958)

The next afternoon, I found myself on the Cabot & Sons pier. King was at the desk in his cramped office going over a stack of paperwork as I stepped inside and cleared my throat.

"Well, as I live and breathe, it's none other than Archie Goodwin, the boy detective, in person!" he said with a grin, standing and sticking out a hand. "What brings you to this humble corner of the mighty metropolis, shamus? Are you slumming?"

"It seems to me your so-called 'humble corner' is pretty pleasant on this summer day," I replied. "A gentle breeze wafting off the great river and a cloudless sky. What more could a man want out of life?"

"Let me count the ways," King shot back. "For starters, the Giants are at the Polo Grounds this fine afternoon, and I could be in a front-row box seat with a beer and a frank. How's that for starters?"

"Point taken, Charlie. Still, you can't call this a bad existence."

"Oh, it's okay," he said with a grin. "Who am I to complain? But I'm guessing you didn't come all the way out here to talk about the weather."

"You've found me out. I'm wondering if you have heard about any funny business along the North River docks lately."

"I haven't, I'm happy to tell you, and I have damned good contacts up and down this stretch of the river. Oh, some months back there was a ruckus three piers south of here over a longshoreman who was caught rifling the coat pockets of other members of his crew in the locker room. He got sacked and that was that, though. Do you know something I don't?"

"Not really. We're looking into the disappearance of a man who had spent time in McCready's bar over on Tenth Avenue."

Charlie scowled. "I'm also happy to say that most of my crew here are family men and don't hang out in that place. Some of the roughest customers working on the docks are regulars there, though. Is the guy who disappeared a dockworker?"

"No, just an ordinary joe who played cards at McCready's," I told him, avoiding any further detail.

"Well, if I hear anything suspicious, I will give you a call. I've still got your card somewhere in this messy desk, and I assume you're still working with Nero Wolfe over on West Thirty-Fifth?"

"Yep, some things never change, Charlie. Hope you get to a Giants game soon. They're looking pretty good this year."

"Unfortunately, so are those damned Dodgers," he said ruefully, turning back to his paperwork.

CHAPTER 6

By the time I returned to the brownstone, Wolfe was upstairs indulging himself in the afternoon session with the orchids. When he came down at six and rang for beer, I looked up from typing some of his correspondence. "Want a report on my visit to the docks? Not much to tell."

"It can wait until later, when the others arrive," he said, signing the letters I had already typed and stacked on his desk blotter.

"How is Carl Willis working out in the plant rooms? Any improvement?" I asked.

"Still adequate," Wolfe replied. "He follows orders, although he could hardly be termed a self-starter. He needs a great deal of direction."

"You probably are intimidating to the poor fellow."

"Me, intimidating?" Wolfe raised his eyebrows and assumed an expression of shocked innocence. I thought of several responses but passed on all of them. My mind already was focused on dinner, which was to be curried beef roll with celery and cantaloupe salad, followed by blueberry pie à la mode, and at that point, I was not about to point out my boss's irascibilities to him.

All three of our regular operatives were prompt, arriving at the brownstone by eight forty-five. Like veteran cast members in a play, they all knew their places: Saul settled into the red leather chair at the end of Wolfe's desk, while Fred and Orrie took the yellow chairs in front of the desk.

I played bartender, serving scotch on the rocks to Saul and Orrie and beer to Fred, who felt that by drinking what our host did, he honored him. I didn't have the heart to tell him Wolfe did not care one way or the other. Even among longtime associates, Wolfe liked to make his entrance after everyone was seated. Besides, I knew where he was: in the kitchen with Fritz, planning—and probably arguing over—the lunches and dinners for the next several days.

At nine on the button, Wolfe walked in and sat, with Fritz trailing him with beer for him and Fred and chilled glasses on a tray. "Gentleman, thank you all for coming," he said as he popped the cap off one of the bottles and poured. "Saul, what have you learned?"

"Not a lot, Mr. Wolfe," Panzer said. "As instructed, I walked up to Sid, Harvey, and Chester as they were playing pinochle, and they wanted to know if I played bridge. I said I did, and they were glad to see me. I asked who was normally their fourth, and they mentioned Theodore—or rather, 'Ted.'

"I casually asked where he was, and they said they didn't know, that they were puzzled about his absence. I then told them I occasionally played in some pick-up bridge games in that general neighborhood, and I remembered meeting Ted at one of those games. I went on to describe Theodore, and they all told me that was him, all right.

"'Seems like a pleasant fellow, well-mannered,' I said, to which I got unanimous agreement. 'The last couple times he played with us, though, he seemed to be distracted,' Sid commented. 'It was as if for some reason he was nervous around the longshoremen who hang out in McCready's. I happen to think they're a bunch of rough customers, but I have no idea what they might have against Ted.'

"They didn't seem to bother us when we were playing," Saul went on, "although they—at least the ones playing pool—made a few snide remarks to us as they passed by on their way to and from the bar."

"Such as?" Wolfe posed.

"'Why don't you try a man's game?' and 'What a damned waste of time!' We all ignored them, of course, which took a lot of the wind out of their sails," Saul said. "I brought up Theodore one more time during the evening, but none of the three had anything else to add except to hope that his absence didn't mean something bad had happened to him. I'm sorry I wasn't able to come up with anything more."

"You did as well as you possibly could," said Wolfe, who has always felt that Saul can do no wrong. "What about you, Fred?"

Durkin, who is always uneasy around the boss, cleared his throat. "I sat at the bar for more than two hours, and I nursed my beers. Over that time, four . . . no, *five* guys sat next to me, on one side or the other, and they all seemed to be dockworkers.

"I mentioned that I hadn't been in McCready's recently, and I was surprised to see that a card game was going on in the back room. 'Aw, I don't know why Mac allows it,' one on a barstool said, referring to the bartender, who I figure must be McCready himself. 'If they just got rid of that damned card table, they'd have room for another pocket billiard table in there. There's always a waiting list to shoot pool.'

"I asked if it was always the same guys who played bridge, and nobody seemed to know, or maybe it was the case that they just didn't care. It was obvious that the regulars resented the card games."

"Was there any rough stuff done against the card players, Fred?"

"I asked that question to a couple of the regulars myself, Archie, and they acted like they wouldn't hurt a flea, let alone somebody playing bridge."

"Perhaps it is a case of protesting too much," Wolfe said, turning to me with a slight dip of the chin, a signal it now was my turn. I should mention that whenever we all gather to report, Wolfe prefers that Orrie Cather go last because he knows he likes to take his time once he has center stage.

I gave my brief and essentially bland summary of having talked to Charlie King and said, "Sorry, but my cupboard is bare. If Charlie doesn't know of trouble on the docks, it's likely that nobody does."

Wolfe nodded to Orrie, who leaned forward in his chair with a grin. "That place where Horstmann's been living on Tenth Avenue may look peaceful and ordinary from the outside, but something funny's going on in there, and I just can't seem to figure it out."

"Try, Orrie," Wolfe urged.

"Yes, sir. Well, I talked to nine of the residents," he said, pulling out his notebook and flipping some pages. "Almost all of them seemed . . . I don't know, secretive."

"That sounds like typical New Yorkers to me," Saul put in. "Anybody who rings their doorbell makes them suspicious by nature."

"Maybe so," Orrie conceded, "but I made it clear right from start that I wasn't selling anything. I was upfront and told them I was a friend of Mr. Horstmann in 412. I showed each of them his photo and said I hadn't heard anything from him for days, which was very unusual, as we usually talked almost daily. Three people slammed the door in my face, four more said they had never seen or heard of Horstmann—even though one of those lived right next door to him. And the others just shook their heads and looked at me blankly. One of those two, an older woman, had a look of fright and kept shaking her head."

"Maybe your appearance scared her," I said.

"Very funny, Archie. I was wearing my best suit, and I went out of my way to be extremely polite. After I'd rung all the buzzers in the place and talked to—or tried to talk to—everyone who answered, I then went downstairs to the street-level apartment of the super, an underfed and mopey guy named Bauer, who also seemed like he didn't want to say much when I asked him if he had any idea what might have happened to Theodore.

"'You *do* know Mr. Horstmann, don't you?' I asked Bauer, and he said, word for word, 'Yes, I met him, of course, and I've seen him a couple of other times, but it's really hard to keep track of everyone here, because of all the turnover.'

"'Why is that? Is it because people don't like the conditions here?' I shot back, and he became very defensive. 'Oh no, this is a very well-run building, no rats, no burglaries, none of the tenants ever causing trouble,' he told me, but he was really sweating, to the point where his shirt was showing stains under the arms."

"Not a pretty picture," Wolfe remarked sourly.

"No, sir. After that, I talked to people in the three businesses at street level in the building. None of them said they recognized Horstmann by his picture, although I was suspicious of the man in the dry cleaners, who gave one quick look at the photo and shook his head vigorously—a little too vigorously for my money. The two barbers in the shop claimed they had never seen Horstmann before, and it was the same with the guy behind the counter in the deli. I wouldn't vouch for any of them one way or the other.

"Then I went across the street to a small grocery and showed the picture to the Italian owner, who just shrugged and said he'd never seen Horstmann. And he said more than that . . ." added Orrie, who loved to be dramatic. "'That place over there,' he told me, gesturing to the Elmont, 'is bad, very bad, *cattivo*.'

"I asked what he meant, and he muttered, 'Not nice people, not nice at all.' When I pressed him, he clammed up like he had said too much. I would have kept at it, but just then two women entered, and the *paisano* got in one big hurry to wait on them so he could get away from me. I hung around for a few more minutes, but other shoppers kept coming in, so I figured I wasn't going to squeeze any more out of him, especially the way he looked out of the corner of his eye at me like I was a plainclothes cop ready to haul him in for an all-night grilling."

"You, a plainclothes cop?" Saul said, trying to sound shocked.

"Hey, why not? I was almost on the force once, you know, and I would have been if wasn't for that damned Lieutenant Rowcliff, who hates all private investigators and who blocked my application."

The mention of George Rowcliff was enough to unite us. Saul rolled his eyes, Fred made a gagging sound, and Wolfe scowled, saying, "The man is a disgrace to the department. Be happy you got turned down, Orrie, or you might have ended up working under him."

"That is a good point," Orrie replied. "What do you think about what I just told you, Mr. Wolfe?"

"It suggests more work lies ahead for us, particularly in that building where Theodore had been residing."

"Tell us what you want, sir," Saul said. "I believe I can speak for all of us in saying that we are willing to put everything else aside to hunt for whoever attacked Theodore."

"Yeah, I don't think we even have to take a vote on that," Fred added, looking around and seeing nods from Orrie and me.

"Just so. You will be hearing from me through Archie, almost surely as soon as tomorrow," Wolfe said, rising and heading toward the elevator. His day in the office had ended.

CHAPTER 7

After breakfast the next day, I sat in the office with coffee, slitting open the morning mail, stacking it on Wolfe's desk blotter, and filing the orchid germination records that our new man in the plant rooms, Willis, had left on my desk while I was in the kitchen devouring Fritz's wheat cakes, sausage, and eggs. Willis may not be as good with the orchids as Theodore, but his handwriting is a damn sight better.

Just as I rose to get a java refill in the kitchen, the phone rang, and I was greeted by the voice of Lon Cohen of the *New York Gazette*. "I fondly remember the good old days," he said with what was meant to be a heart-rending sigh.

"Meaning what, oh, ink-stained wretch?"

"Meaning that I never hear from you anymore, other than at our weekly poker games, from which I invariably walk away with more shekels than you do."

"Where is all this gibberish leading?"

"Gibberish, is it? I'm just thinking back to the good old days when you would phone me if you had something newsworthy."

"I don't believe I'm aware of anything newsworthy at present, my noble scrivener."

"You don't consider the orchid-tender to a world-famous detective lingering in a coma in a hospital to be newsworthy?"

"You seem to have eyes and ears everywhere."

"Damn right," said Cohen, who has no title I'm aware of at America's fifth-largest newspaper, although he has the ear of the publisher and, based on what I have seen and heard, he issues orders to the *Gazette*'s editor and also has a big part in deciding what each day's headline story will be.

"Okay, so your intrepid snoops have found out about Theodore Horstmann. So what?"

"So what?" Lon fired back. "We have also learned that he was mugged—hell, more than mugged; he was beaten almost to death. Everybody knows that Nero Wolfe has enemies—lots of them—and some of the lowlifes that he's nailed, often with the help of the police of course, would do anything to get revenge on him, including hurting those close to him. What do you know about this, Archie? You can't hold out on me."

"Right now, I know very little, other than what you already seem to know. Theodore, who moved out of the brownstone a few months ago, has been living in a building on Tenth Avenue but is still working for Wolfe, helping tend the orchids a good part of each day, just like before. We have no idea why he was beaten. He showed up at our door the other night and collapsed, saying nothing. He's been in the hospital in a coma ever since."

"I've gotta believe, Archie, that you and Wolfe and every other operative you can get your hands on, Panzer included, are working on this."

"Okay, I will concede you that. But here's the situation: As far as we've been able to tell, no one, including whoever beat him, knows whether he's even alive or not, and we plan to keep it that way. Our investigation—and yes, Saul's in on it, as well as Durkin and Cather—is proceeding as if we believe Theodore is missing. The last thing we need right now is for the *Gazette,* or any other paper or radio or a TV station, to report that he's in the hospital."

"That's asking a lot, Archie."

"Maybe so. But we've always played straight with each other, and I can speak for Nero Wolfe when I tell you that if you sit on this now, you'll get an exclusive later. We've delivered in the past, you can't deny that."

I could hear exhaling on the other end of the line. "All right," Lon said, "we'll back off—for now. But I'm counting on you and Wolfe to give the *Gazette* whatever you've got before anybody else."

"Do you want to add up the times we've given you an exclusive?" I barked into the phone. "I've got the records on file if you've got the time to hear me out."

"Okay, okay, you've made your point," Lon said. "I have to go, there's a big fire over in Long Island City that looks like it could burn down a city block and maybe a lot more." Before I could respond, he hung up, as he had done so often in the past. Lon has three telephones on his desk, so even though he is at least ten floors above the *Gazette*'s newsroom near the publisher's office, he probably is better plugged into the events of the day than most of the paper's reporters. I had got him off our backs—at least for the present.

When Wolfe came down from the plant rooms at eleven and rang for beer, I swiveled to face him and reported my conversation with our newspaper friend.

"Pfui! That was to be expected," he said. "Mr. Cohen can be most persistent, sometimes to an irritating degree, although he also has been helpful to us many times in the past, supplying us with information possessed only by newspapers and their employees."

"You might call Lon a mixed bag," I said.

"I would not," Wolfe sniffed.

"Okay, Boss," I said, getting back at him by using the b-word, which he hates. "Where do we go from here?"

"It would be helpful to learn more about Theodore's neighbors. From what Orrie was able to learn, there seems to be a great deal of secrecy pervading the building, although he has a tendency to picture situations as more dramatic than they are."

"That's true," I said, "but as Saul pointed out, New Yorkers are suspicious by nature, so the reactions Orrie got seem predictable to me. Bear in mind that you have never had to ring doorbells and get cold shoulders from people who don't want to be disturbed, for whatever reasons."

Wolfe grunted but said nothing. He dislikes being lectured to, even when he realizes the lecturer has made a point, as was the case here. Then a frown dominated in his face, and I sensed that trouble was coming my way. I was correct.

"Archie, call Mr. Cohen back. Tell him we need a favor."

"Lon may not want to speak to me right now. He felt I was being uncooperative."

"Use your powers of persuasion," Wolfe went on as the frown deepened. "See what our newspaperman—and his *Gazette*'s files—can tell us about Theodore's apartment building. And also find out if there have been untoward activities on the docks and in that bar."

I reluctantly redialed Lon's number, and when he heard it was me, he said, "So, the prodigal son comes crawling back.

Okay, welcome back . . . I guess. What have you got to tell me about Theodore Horstmann?"

"It's what I hope we can learn from you. We would like to know what your files contain about the building Theodore has been living in. It's five stories and has merchants on the street level, a dry cleaner, a deli, and a barbershop." I gave him the address on Tenth Avenue.

"Archie, this may surprise you, but I have got far more pressing things to do than to drop everything and serve as your research assistant." I knew I was going to get grief from Lon, so I let him ramble on.

"You know that fire in Long Island City that I mentioned before? Well, it's still going on, and even spreading because of the wind. And do you know what people phoning in to us are worried about? Not that families or businesses could get displaced, but that the big Pepsi-Cola sign facing the East River and Manhattan might be threatened. How's that for getting your priorities turned upside down?"

"Yeah, it's pathetic, all right."

"Glad that we agree on something today," Lon said. "I'll call down to the morgue and see what we've got, if anything, on that Tenth Avenue address and check with our guy who covers the Hell's Kitchen area, all the way to the piers."

"Speaking of the piers, we'd also like to know if there's been any funny business along the docks."

"It that so? Does this also relate to your man Horstmann?"

"Could be. And while you're at it, has there been any trouble your guys have heard about at McCready's Bar, also on Tenth Avenue?"

"Let me get this straight, Archie. You want to know anything out of the ordinary that we can discover about: one) that Tenth Avenue apartment building; two) the North River docks; and three) McCready's Bar? By the way, just what do the docks and that saloon have to do with Horstmann?"

"That has yet to be determined."

"Ever the man of mystery. It sounds like you want us to do your work for you," Lon grumped. "Whatever would you and Wolfe do without the *Gazette*?"

"I've often asked myself the same question, along with another one: Whatever would the *Gazette* do without Wolfe's brain and my brawn?"

The reply I got was a snort, which was followed by a click. The line had gone dead.

CHAPTER 8

Wolfe heard my half of the conversation with Lon, which was enough for him to know the call's substance. "All right, what is our next step?" I asked.

"Pending any information we receive from Mr. Cohen, I believe it would be helpful if you were to dwell in Theodore's apartment for a period."

"Me, live over on Tenth Avenue? And just how do you define *a period*?"

Those damned folds appeared on Wolfe's face again. He was having too much fun moving me around like a chess piece. "Your length of stay, as I just stated, may depend upon what we learn from Mr. Cohen."

"How can I function in the office if I'm bunking blocks from here?"

"I would expect you to be in the office during much of the working day. That would leave you enough time in your temporary abode to discover whether the place is as secretive as Orrie seems to believe."

"It's possible there are no openings in that place," I told him.

"There doesn't need to be any openings, Archie. You can go to the building superintendent, Mr. Bauer. Tell him you are Theodore's cousin from out of town who has come to New York to help find him. You will ask if you can stay in his apartment for the time being."

"And that I will also pay the rent in his absence, right?"

"Correct. It seems probable he will welcome you on those terms."

"Any other instructions?"

"Meet as many of the building's residents as you can without appearing overly inquisitive. Let us discover how perceptive Orrie is."

To say I was unhappy with the assignment would be an understatement, but as I stated earlier, Theodore has for many years been very much a part of our family in the brownstone. This was no time for me to balk.

I went up to my room, packed a suitcase with the essentials for what I hoped would be a short stay, then went to the dining room for lunch, which was a mushroom and almond omelet. Because business is never discussed during meals, no words were exchanged about my imminent move up to Tenth Avenue. But once we went into the office with coffee, I turned to Wolfe.

"Okay, I'm ready to go. How much of each day do you want me to spend in that place?"

"Enough to interact with the building's tenants and take their measure," he said, setting down another of his current books, *Closing the Ring*, by Winston Churchill. "However, as I said, I expect you to be here for a portion of each day. Your *raison d'être* for residing on Tenth Avenue is to search for your relative, so it would not be unusual for you to be gone from that place for hours."

Heaven forbid Wolfe would be without my services for any length of time. This way, he could have the best of both worlds: me in the brownstone available for myriad duties, and me on Tenth Avenue in the Hell's Kitchen neighborhood to learn what I could about what manner of people live in a tired and less-than-luxurious five-story building.

After I finished typing letters Wolfe had dictated the previous day, I doctored one of the ersatz blank driver's license forms we kept on hand for contingencies, said goodbye to the detective and Fritz, and set off on foot, suitcase in hand, for what was to become my new and, as I hoped, *very* temporary dwelling place.

The super's apartment was the only residential unit on the first floor, its door at the back of the unadorned lobby. I pushed the buzzer.

After less than a minute, the door popped open, and a gaunt specimen answering to Orrie's description squinted up at me. "Yeah?"

"Hello, are you the building superintendent?"

"That's me, Erwin Bauer," he said, jabbing a thumb at a con-cave chest covered by a soiled undershirt.

"Very nice to meet you. I am the cousin of one of your ten-ants, Ted Horstmann, who as you probably know is missing."

"Yeah, yeah, so I heard," he said, shaking his head as if in disbelief. "So sorry, so sorry. I can't imagine what could have happened to him. I didn't know him all that well, but he seemed like a very polite man, and rather quiet."

"That's him, all right. I have come in from out of town, and if you have no objection, I would like to stay in his apartment for a few days while I look for him. And I would of course pay the rent for as long as I stay."

Bauer looked around, as if thinking my proposal over. Then he chewed on his upper lip. "Uh . . . yes, that would be all right. What is your name?"

"Art."

He nodded. "And your last name?"

"Horstmann, of course."

He broke into a smile and seemed relieved. "Yes, of course, Mr. Horstmann, of course. I will show you to your uncle's apartment and give you a key."

"Thank you. Does he owe you any money now? I'll be happy to pay if he does, or even pay something in advance."

"I believe that he is paid up, at least for the balance of this month."

"When more rent is due, I trust you will inform me."

"I will, yes, sir, I will." I believe my eagerness to pay prevented the super from asking for identification. I could have provided him with a driver's license listing me as Arthur Horstmann of Defiance, Ohio, but I was happy to leave it in my pocket.

"Do you have a lot of turnover here?" I asked Bauer.

"No, not really. Many of the tenants have been in the building for several years." I found his answer interesting, contrasting it with what he had told Orrie, but I said nothing. I also found it intriguing that Bauer made no mention that anyone (Orrie) had been asking about the "missing" tenant.

The super handed me a key and we went up in the creaky elevator. He opened the door to 412 with his skeleton key and led the way in. "Mr. Horstmann seems to be very neat," Bauer said, looking around and smiling. "That is good to see."

"Yes, my uncle has always been very tidy," I told him, playing the role of the loyal and concerned nephew who was in the unit for the first time. "I only hope that he will be found soon and can return here. He told me that he liked this apartment."

"Where do you come from?" Bauer asked.

"Ohio," I replied, which actually was true, if you were to go back a number of years. "Everyone back home is of course very worried about my uncle."

Bauer nodded, wearing a somber expression. "Very sad, very sad." He looked up at me and shook his head, indicating he had nothing more to say. I thanked him and said I would settle in and begin the search for "Uncle Ted." He backed out into the hall, bowing as if playing the role of a servant. The act was not convincing.

The apartment looked as it did on my earlier visit—hardly a surprise. I unpacked quickly and put my clothes in drawers and on hangers and my shaving kit in the bathroom, in case Bauer or anyone else might decide to snoop around.

I left my new "home" and walked down rather than taking the elevator, in hopes of running into other residents in the halls. At the second-floor landing, I did indeed meet a heavy-set man of about sixty, who also was headed downstairs. "Nice weather we're having, isn't it?" I said. The response was a muttered "yeh," and not a word more. So much for one not-so-friendly neighbor.

I stepped outside and took stock. I did not want to spoil Wolfe by returning to the brownstone after such a brief time away, so I crossed to the other side of Tenth Avenue and asked myself what Saul Panzer would do in this situation. He has the ability to blend in with his surroundings, which I then tried to do by easing into a narrow gangway between two buildings, all but out-of-sight to passersby. I stayed there for twenty-two minutes by my watch, and in that time, six people entered Theodore's building and five came out.

They all were men and all were white, and not one of them looked to be under forty. This was a nondescript bunch, neither tall nor short, thin nor fat, and not particularly welldressed, mostly wearing open-collared shirts, no suits and ties. If they had one trait uniting them, it was a grim expression, which I found to be strange. One would think that on such a sunny and breezy summer day, a few of these faces would have been graced with a smile. Of those who left the building, one came across the street, dodging taxis and bicycle messengers in the process, and entered the Italian grocery store that Orrie had mentioned in his report. He emerged ten minutes later with a bulging sack that had a long loaf of bread sticking out of it. It reminded me of similar bread I had seen pedestrians and bicyclists carrying when Lily and I had been in Paris the previous summer.

One man who ventured forth from the Elmont quickly spun around, turning his back to a squad car, which, with sirens blaring, was tearing by. I also noticed that another tenant walked directly across the street and into McCready's, hardly surprising as it was the nearest bar to the apartment building. After a few more minutes, I decided I was wasting my time as a watchman and went into McCready's myself.

The bar was lightly patronized, with only a few stools occupied, and the back room was free both of card players and pool sharks. I ordered a scotch and water from a young bartender and noticed that the man I had seen crossing the street from Theodore's building was in an earnest and whispering but facially expressive conversation with the older barkeep, whom I assumed to be McCready. They huddled for several minutes with their foreheads almost touching before the bartender patted the other man on the shoulder in a paternal gesture, and I watched as he walked out wearing a sad expression.

I tried without success to strike up a conversation with a burly man two stools away, but he was more interested in watching the Yankees run up a big score on the Philadelphia Athletics.

Figuring that my afternoon had been a waste of time, I walked south to the brownstone.

By the time I got back, Wolfe was upstairs with the orchids. As I got settled at my desk in the office, Fritz entered. "You just missed a call from Mr. Cohen, Archie. He would like you to telephone him."

Lon picked up on the first ring and barked his name into the mouthpiece. I responded in like manner, but not as loud.

"Well, Mr. Ace Detective, so far it seems like you may be on the proverbial wild goose chase, based on early returns from the provinces," Cohen said. "First off, we haven't got much on that Tenth Avenue building, which happens to be called the Elmont. The last time it made any kind of news in our pages was almost six years ago, when a short piece reported that the place was cited for what the building department termed 'unsanitary conditions.'"

"Meaning rats?"

"Our piece didn't say, although that's often the case. Anyway, the management company, which is based over in Jersey City, promised to address the problem. A note in the Elmont morgue file from one of our reporters noted that the building was given a thumbs-up by the department three months later, so either they cleaned things up or bribed somebody, which is always a possibility.

"As for the docks," Lon went on, "we haven't had much at all lately. A couple of fights among longshoremen and a stowaway from Austria who was found on a freighter that came in from Rotterdam. That's the sum of it over the last couple of years."

"And what about that bar, McCready's?" I asked.

"Nothing much there, either. The place has had a few minor brawls, of course, but that hardly makes it unique among the saloons in our fair metropolis."

"I gather a guy named McCready runs the bar."

"Yeah, Liam McCready, who our reporter said came over from Ireland early on during the war, even before we got into it. He had inherited the place after the death of an uncle, who had operated it since the repeal of Prohibition. The nephew is now an American citizen. McCready was quoted as being the owner in a piece we ran involving a fight in the bar about two years back. He said, 'I was terribly sorry that a little disagreement got out of hand, and I promise I will prevent anything like this from ever happening in the future.'"

"Sounds like an upstanding gentleman."

"So it would seem," Lon said. "In any case, that's the last time the joint has made it into print in the *Gazette*. That's all we have for you. You got anything for me?"

"Nothing, and we still don't know who attacked Theodore—or why."

"But once you've made a discovery, I am sure that I will be the first to hear, right?"

"You know me, Lon."

"That's what I'm afraid of," he said, signing off.

CHAPTER 9

Not five minutes after my call with Lon Cohen had ended, the phone rang. It was Doc Vollmer.

"As of this morning, there is no change in Theodore's condition, Archie."

"If you were to give odds on his survival, what would they be?"

"I am not in the business of giving odds," the doctor said stiffly. "But the positive news is that Theodore's vital signs are good. I was in his room yesterday when his sister walked in, and I detected a glimmer of recognition from him, although I admit that may have been wishful thinking on my part."

I thanked Vollmer for the report, and just as I hung up, Wolfe came into the office from his afternoon session with the orchids. I filled him in on my afternoon on Tenth Avenue and Vollmer's call.

"I would like to see Theodore's sister," he said as he rang for beer. "See if she can be here tomorrow at eleven."

I had only met Horstmann's widowed sister, Frieda, once, several years ago, when she stopped by the brownstone to pick him up and take him out to dinner on his birthday. It was he who usually visited her.

"I'm not sure I will be able to reach her, but I'll try," I told Wolfe, knowing that she would be spending a lot of time shuttling between her home in Hoboken and the Manhattan hospital where Theodore lay in a coma. I dialed the New Jersey phone number we had on file, and, much to my surprise, she answered.

"It's Archie Goodwin, Mrs. Mueller," I said, pleased I could remember her married name. "First, we are so sorry about Theodore and what has happened. Second, Nero Wolfe wonders if you could come to his home on West Thirty-Fifth Street tomorrow morning at eleven o'clock."

"Oh, Mr. Goodwin . . . pardon me . . . I am out-of-breath," she said, panting. "I just walked in the door from visiting my brother to hear the telephone ringing."

"Take your time."

"No, no, I am all right. You say Mr. Wolfe wishes to see me?"

"Yes, if it does not interfere with your trips to the hospital."

"They are very generous with their visiting hours. I have only been to Mr. Wolfe's residence once, a few years ago. Can you give me the address?"

I did, telling her that I remembered meeting her on her lone trip to the brownstone. My memory was of a thick-set but not fat woman of middle age who was every bit as unemotional and taciturn as her brother. She had not seemed unfriendly, but rather acted extremely reserved, a trait that clearly ran in the family. I told her that she would be expected in the morning, and we ended the call.

I pivoted to Wolfe, who was just starting popping open one of the beers Fritz had brought in. "Frieda Mueller will be here, as requested. What do you hope to learn from her?"

"I don't know, perhaps nothing. But we would do well to express our concern for her brother. I believe her to be his only living relative."

"Yes, she and her husband had no children. You may recall that he died at least ten years ago. You may also remember that Theodore had never liked the man."

"Yes, I do recall his negative reaction to his brother-in-law. What man ever approves of his sister's choice in a spouse?"

"You make a good point," I said. "I have two sisters, and I feel they each could have done better in picking a husband. But then, I don't recall either of them asking my opinion on the matter, maybe because they knew what my reaction would be. Back to business: After dinner, I'll be going back to Tenth Avenue. Do you have any instructions?"

"Nothing specific. I expect you will meet more of your neighbors the longer you dwell in that abode. I shall be interested in your observations."

"Yeah, me, too. Although I'm not excited by your words, 'the longer you dwell . . .' I do not plan to dwell all that long in that five-story pile of bricks-and-mortar up in the heart of Hell's Kitchen."

"You are making this sacrifice, if it can be so termed, to help us learn why Theodore now lies in a hospital bed fighting for his life," Wolfe said.

"Okay, okay, you are correct as usual. While I return to my new—and temporary—home, what plans do you have for the members of our team?"

"Telephone Saul, and see if he is available to play bridge once more with the gentlemen in the back room at McCready's,"

Wolfe replied. "For the present, we have no need for the services of Fred or Orrie."

I reached Saul, who said he would drop in tonight and see if the trio of card players in the saloon needed a fourth for bridge again. Then as planned, following dinner, I walked over to Tenth Avenue and headed north to see what I could learn about my fellow roomers.

Once again, rather than riding the elevator, I used the stairs in the hope that I would run into one or more of my neighbors in the Elmont. At the second-floor landing, I did come upon a hunched-over man of uncertain age with a two-day growth of beard who was shuffling his way down the stairs.

"Hello, my name is Art Horstmann. I haven't met you," I said in my friendliest tone as I stuck out a hand. "I am temporarily staying up in 412, which is the apartment of my uncle, Ted Horstmann. Do you happen to know him?" He shook his head and attempted to ease past me on the narrow stairway, but I blocked the way without seeming to be hostile. Finally, realizing he would have to speak to break the stalemate, he said, "No, no, I do not know him." Hardly a lot of words, but enough to tell that he spoke with an accent, possibly German or Dutch, or maybe Swiss. Wolfe, with his knowledge of languages, would have nailed it right away.

"And what is your name, sir?" I asked to his back as he continued down the stairs without looking back. I received no reply.

In the fourth-floor hallway, I got lucky, if you want to call it that. Another man of middle age, this one lanky and wearing glasses, was just stepping out of his room. I repeated my introduction and added that we were almost next-door neighbors. My answer was a blank stare, followed by hand gestures toward his open-and-closed mouth that seemed to indicate he was unable to speak—or chose not to. A code of silence in more ways than one.

For want of anything else to do, I decided to cross Tenth Avenue to McCready's for a drink. The bar was crowded, and through the door to the back room, I could see the bridge game, complete with Saul Panzer, who apparently had been the bidder and looked to be raking in tricks. I found a stool near the front door and parked, ordering a scotch.

As I looked along the length of the bar toward the back, I noticed that the lanky, bespectacled character I had just run into at the Elmont appeared to be in an animated conversation with none other than McCready. So much for the man's inability to speak. There was no question that when Orrie Cather said "something funny's going on" in the Elmont, he knew of what he spoke.

CHAPTER 10

Nothing of further interest transpired that night, either at McCready's or in the apartment building. The next morning, I got up at the usual time and after my ablutions, I walked a block north on Tenth Avenue to a coffee shop I had patronized in previous trips through the neighborhood. I sat at the crowded counter and had a plate of scrambled eggs, sausage, and hash browns, along with orange juice and coffee. It was so-so grub, but then, I have been spoiled by years of eating Fritz Brenner's superb breakfasts. When this enforced absence from the brownstone ended, I made myself a promise to tell Fritz how much I appreciate him.

Returning to the Elmont, I failed to meet a single neighbor, not that I had learned anything from those I had previously run into. Glad for the chance to stretch my legs on a pleasant morning, I walked south to Thirty-Fifth Street and entered the brownstone almost a half-hour before Theodore's sister was due.

"Would you like coffee, Archie?" Fritz asked as I settled in at my desk and paged through the stack of mail that he had put on my blotter.

"I would, yes. And Fritz, I might as tell you now instead of waiting until I move back here: You are a true gem."

I thought he was going to tear up, but his Swiss reserve took hold, and he smiled, bowed slightly, and did a crisp about-face, heading back to the kitchen to get my coffee. While waiting for Wolfe's descent from the plant rooms, I opened the morning mail and wrote checks for the gas, telephone, electric, grocery, and beer bills.

My watch read ten fifty-six when the doorbell rang. Through the one-way glass in the front door, I saw the impassive face of a woman I recognized from our one meeting several years ago—Theodore Horstmann's sister.

"Good morning, Mrs. Mueller," I said, holding open the door for her. She wore a lightweight black coat and a no-nonsense hat, also black, and clutched a purse tightly with both hands as if fearing someone was about to snatch it.

"You are . . . Mr. Goodwin, aren't you?" she asked in a hesitant tone.

"I am. It has been a long time since we saw each other." I helped her off with her coat, hung it on the hall tree, and steered her down the hall to the office. "Can I get you coffee?" I asked as I gestured her to the red leather chair.

"No, thank you, Mr. Goodwin. I already had—" She stopped talking as Wolfe entered the office and gave her a brief nod. "Mrs. Mueller, thank you so much for coming. Would you like something to drink, coffee perhaps?"

"I had breakfast and coffee at the hospital this morning," she told him.

"Before we go any further, how is Theodore today?"

"No improvement." Like her brother, Frieda Mueller used words sparingly, and her lack of facial expression was similar to his as well. She seemed to betray no emotion whatever.

"Had you talked to Theodore in the days before he was attacked?" Wolfe asked as he rang for beer.

"We usually spoke by telephone two or three times a week," she replied. "Yes, I do believe that we talked the day before . . . before what happened to him."

"Did he say anything that might suggest he had particular concerns?"

She waited several seconds before responding. "Theodore said where he was living was comfortable, but he had told me that before. He had also said in an earlier call that the people in his new building were not friendly. They barely answered when he said anything to them in the hallways."

"Does your brother speak German?"

"We both do," Frieda said. "Our parents were born over there and spoke German at home when we were growing up in New Jersey."

"Did Theodore describe any other impressions he had of his neighbors at the Elmont, or any traits they had?" Wolfe asked.

"He had said once that he thought many of them seemed to be foreign, and I remember telling him that did not sound surprising to me. There are also a large number of foreign-born people in my building over in Hoboken. Many displaced persons—they are often called 'DPs' but I don't like that word—have come here from Europe since the end of the war."

"Three years ago," Wolfe said, "President Truman signed an act that allowed thousands of persons who had lost their homes during the war to immigrate to the United States, and great numbers of them have come to New York, in many cases because they have relatives here. Did your brother think that was the case with those around him?"

"He didn't say, but he felt uneasy, as though he were an outsider there."

"Perhaps because he was still new to the building," Wolfe posed.

"I don't think so," Frieda Mueller said. "Others had arrived there since Theodore had moved in, and he said they seemed to be accepted."

"Did he say what languages were spoken in the Elmont?" I asked.

She shook her head. "That was something that puzzled him. He told me it was as though no one in the building wanted to speak. At least three times when he tried to greet a neighbor, he got nothing more than a shake of the head. No words."

"It is possible some of these newcomers are embarrassed about their lack of English," I said.

Frieda pursed her lips but said nothing, which may have been her way of disagreeing with me. She was every bit as tight-lipped as her brother. Words apparently were not thrown around casually in the Horstmann household when she and Theodore were young.

Wolfe, sensing the conversation had reached a stalemate, changed course. "I understand Theodore had taken up bridge," he said. "Did he talk to you about that?"

She sniffed. "Yes, he mentioned it. It sounded like a waste of time to me, but I did not tell him what I thought. It's his life."

"I understand he played in a bar called McCready's near where he lived. Did he say anything about the type of people in there?"

Another sniff. "He did not have to say anything, it was obvious. What kind of people could possibly be spending time in a saloon? I am just glad that our parents are not alive to see what has happened."

"Do you believe what befell Theodore had anything to do with the people in McCready's?"

"I do not know what to believe. He did mention that he thought there was some sort of funny business going on in that . . . that place, but he did not get specific. Mr. Wolfe, I am not a rich woman—far from it. And I know from what Theodore has told me that you charge very high fees to your clients. I do have some money put away, though, and I would like to hire you to find out who did this terrible thing to my brother."

"If you please, madam," Wolfe said, holding up a palm. "What has happened to Theodore is a personal affront to me. I plan to investigate what has occurred, and I expect no remuneration whatever."

"Now it is my turn to say please," Frieda replied, leaning forward in her chair. "I want to have an involvement in what you are doing. I must insist that you accept some payment from me."

Wolfe dipped his chin. "Very well. Give me a check for one-hundred dollars, which will make you a full partner in this effort."

She frowned. "That seems like very little."

"Are you familiar with *the widow's mite*?"

Frieda looked as if she had been slapped. "Of course, I am! It appears in both Mark and in Luke. I happen to know my Bible, and probably better than you do."

"Perhaps, madam. Then you are of course aware that true value is not measured by the size of the offering, but rather by the commitment and the earnestness behind that gift."

That seemed to stymie the woman, who unclasped the purse in her lap and drew out a checkbook. "Whom should I make this to?"

"To Nero Wolfe. On the memo line, the words 'for professional services,' will suffice."

She wrote out the check and handed it to Wolfe, who said, "Your contribution amounts to one hundred percent of the cash investment in this case. Mr. Goodwin and I, with the aid of others in our employ, will endeavor to see that your money is well spent. Do you have anything else to tell us about your thoughts regarding what happened to your brother?"

"I do not. As you know, Theodore has never been a rash or an impulsive man, far from it. And he certainly is not an aggressive person by nature. I cannot imagine who would wish to harm my brother."

"I am in agreement with your assessment," Wolfe said, standing. "Mr. Goodwin will keep you apprised of any developments."

Frieda Mueller realized she had been dismissed and rose as Wolfe walked out of the office. I led her down the hall and helped her on with her coat. "Can I get you a taxi?" I asked.

"No, thank you, Mr. Goodwin. I will go to the end of the block, and I should have no trouble flagging one down. I am going back to the hospital."

"You have been doing a lot of traveling between Hoboken and Manhattan," I observed.

"One does what is needed," was her curt reply as she walked down the front steps and headed for Tenth Avenue. When I returned to the office, Wolfe was back at his desk. "The coast is clear," I told him. "Our grim-faced lady has departed."

"She displays many of the characteristics her brother possesses, including brevity, reticence, and the total lack of a sense of humor."

"On top of that, she seems almost as concerned about Theodore's moral condition as his medical one."

"Theodore has rarely discussed any details of his personal life," Wolfe said, "and I have never encouraged his doing so. But on one occasion several years ago, he mentioned his family was religiously conservative, to the point that they eschewed alcohol, card games, dancing, attending the cinema, and many other so-called worldly activities. His father had hoped to become a fundamentalist minister, but financial considerations prevented him from attending a seminary, so he—Theodore's father, that is—became a factory worker. But he remained active in a church, serving in various roles and imposing his rigid moral code upon his family."

"That way of life seems to have stuck with Theodore's sister," I said.

"Indeed, and she clearly disapproves of at least one of her brother's activities."

"Playing bridge."

"Yes. Enough of the lady. You have yet to report on your recent activities on Tenth Avenue."

"My experience so far corroborates what Theodore told his sister about the other roomers at the Elmont, and also what Orrie found in his visit there," I replied. "The residents are private to the point of obsession. They rarely if ever speak to an outsider, i.e., me." I related my experience with the man who feigned to me that he was unable to speak, yet he was seen talking minutes later to the owner of McCready's in what seemed to be a confidential conversation. I also told Wolfe about the mutterer, who finally spit out a few words so that he could get by me. "I realize New Yorkers can be a damned private lot, but the behavior I've seen on more than one occasion borders on the bizarre. Hell, it *is* bizarre," I said.

I started to expand on my comment when the phone rang. It was Saul Panzer; I mouthed his name to Wolfe, who picked up his instrument. "The only time last night that I took a peek at you in the back room," I told Saul, "you looked like you were doing well."

He chuckled. "I got some good cards and even made a slam. I noticed you, too, holding down one end of the bar. Find out anything interesting?"

"Not a lot. How about you?"

"My bridge partner, who happened to be Harvey last night, made a comment I found interesting. He said that 'there seems to be a shift in the patronage of this place. Oh, the pool players still seem to be longshoremen, all right, but over in the bar, there are men who appear foreign, which doesn't bother me at all. That's just an observation, for what it's worth.'

"'Come to think of it, I've noticed that, too,' Sid chimed in. 'And it seems like several of them spend time talking to the owner, McCready, or Mac, as everybody calls him.'"

"Maybe these newcomers to the bar are Irish," I suggested.

"I didn't get that impression from the card players," Saul said. "Their impression was that these new customers were not all that familiar with English."

"Did they suggest possible nationalities?" Wolfe posed.

"I asked them that, sir, and they weren't sure, but they guessed maybe German or Polish. The truth is, none of them, the card players, that is, ever got close enough to these men to hear their conversations, either with one another or with the bar owner."

"It would seem there is a connection between the bar and the residential building across the street," Wolfe said. "Do you concur?"

"If the men McCready always seems to be huddling with happen to live in the Elmont, yeah, there does seem to be a connection, all right. Maybe he sponsors them when they come over from Europe, if indeed they are recent immigrants."

"That would be most benevolent of Mr. McCready," Wolfe pronounced. "Do you think such to be the case?"

"I withhold my vote until more is known about the man who runs the bar," Saul said.

"I would expect such a stance from you," Wolfe said. "It is prudent to be suspicious of the unknown. Do you have any other thoughts, Archie?"

"I'm also curious about the bar's owner, Liam McCready, by name. Saul, as I have already told Mr. Wolfe, all that Lon Cohen was able to learn about him is that he came over here in 1939, after the war had started in Europe but before we entered the fray. He inherited the bar from an uncle who had died. He apparently had no trouble becoming a U.S. citizen."

"Unless you have any objections, I am going to nose around to see what I can learn about Mr. McCready," Saul said.

"Archie and I have no objections whatever," Wolfe said.

That's just like him, casting not only his vote, but mine as well.

CHAPTER 11

I started to give Wolfe some lip about his presumptuous attitude when the telephone rang. It was Charlie King, from the Cabot & Sons Importers pier over on the Hudson. I motioned Wolfe to pick up, mouthing King's name.

"Hi, Archie. When you were over here the other day, I told you everything on the docks seemed to be kosher," Charlie said. "But something happened yesterday. Maybe it's nothing, but . . ."

"Go on," I prompted.

"One of my crewmembers, Ed Marcucci, went to visit a friend of his at the National Export Lines, two piers over. Do you know them?"

"I've heard of the company, but that's the extent of it."

"Well, they've been around for years, like us. Their ships sail to ports from Dover, Hamburg, and Rotterdam on the north to Marseilles, Barcelona, and Genoa on the south. It's a big operation, larger than ours."

"So, what does that have to do with Ed Marcucci?"

"Oh yeah, sorry. Ed has a friend at National named Mel Phipps, and they were going to grab lunch on Eleventh Avenue. Anyway, Ed walked over to National's pier to pick up Phipps, and he noticed there were men getting off a cargo ship that had just docked who didn't look like either crew members or long-shoremen. He asked about them, and Mel pretty much ducked the question."

"This is Nero Wolfe, Mr. King. Does National Export carry passengers on its ships?"

"That's just it—they don't. And that is what Ed found puzzling. That, plus the fact that his friend definitely did not want to talk about these men."

"What did they look like?" I asked.

"Middle-aged, some older, according to Ed," King said. "There were maybe a dozen of them in all, getting off the ship and walking along the pier, being guided toward the office by a couple of National's men. According to Ed, most of them were grim and seemed frightened or suspicious, looking around and blinking like they were being followed."

"Probably DPs," I said. "Poor devils, heaven knows what all they had gone through during the war."

"Did they look undernourished?" Wolfe asked.

"Ed didn't say, although he mentioned that some of them wore clothes that didn't seem to fit."

"If they're being smuggled here, which could be the case, they probably at least got decent grub on the ship," I said. "The question is, how are they going to blend in and avoid getting caught? Truman's act didn't necessarily give *every* displaced person the right to come to the United States."

"Archie, I will keep asking around," King said. "It's damned hard to keep secrets along the docks, although it seems that

National Export has done a pretty good job of it up until now."

After we hung up. I turned to Wolfe. "And now. . . ?"

"Call Mr. Cohen again, and let him know what we have learned."

Lon was going to get tired of hearing from me, but at least this time, I would have something that just might interest him.

"This isn't the first time we've gotten reports of DPs possibly being smuggled into the country," Cohen said when I reached him in the war room that passes as his office high up in the *Gazette* building and filled him in on what we had learned. "I'll have one of our guys look into it," he said. "What's your interest? You still trying to connect those North River piers with your man Horstmann and his beating?"

"Let us say that we are exploring every avenue."

"Swell, thanks for that. By the way, how is Horstmann doing?"

"No change, at least as of yesterday," I said. I didn't bother to mention that his sister had been to see us—and had hired us.

"Speaking of the North River piers," Lon continued, "we got a police report this morning that a floater was found wedged between pilings on the Hudson at about Fifty-Eighth Street. "He'd been shot. A single bullet to the head did the job, efficient, like a mob hit. I thought you'd like to know, given your interest lately in the piers. His name was . . ." I could hear Lon shuffling papers . . . "Here it is, Chester Miller, age sixty-seven, according to papers found on his person. Fat guy and bald, retired postal worker. Name mean anything to you?"

"No," I lied. "How long had he been in the water?"

"Less than a day, the medics said. A dog walker happened to spot him. We'll give it a short item toward the rear of the first section."

"That sounds like an uncommon occurrence."

"Not as uncommon as you would think," Lon said. "Between suicides and mob hits, bodies get fished out of the water often, and in various states of decay."

"This obviously wasn't a suicide, unless he still had the gun in his hand," I remarked.

"The keen mind of the private eye at work once again. It is indeed a wondrous thing to see."

"Kindly spare me your praise. Have your *Gazette* blood-hounds learned any more about Mr.—what, Miller's—death?"

"It is still early in the game, my boy. Is it nothing more than my newsman's innate curiosity, or do I sense some interest from you regarding this man's demise?"

"What interests me is that it happened in the general neighborhood where Theodore had been residing," I said.

"Worth considering, all right. Could be just a coincidence?"

"Maybe. But, as you said, a lot of bodies get pulled out of our town's rivers for one reason or another."

"But those bodies make a much more interesting story when they don't go into the water by choice."

"I can almost see the wheels turning in your exposé-driven newspaperman's mind."

"Now, be honest, Archie. Doesn't a body with a bullet wound to the head make you wonder what caused this to happen?"

"In an academic way, I suppose."

"You, an academic?" Lon snorted. "A pause here, while I cover my mouth with a handkerchief to keep from laughing."

"Go ahead and laugh. As I recall, the only college you ever attended was the school of hard knocks."

"It was a damned good school, Archie. And it taught me to question everything. Right now, in fact, I'm questioning just how much interest you have in this floater, Miller by name. Somehow, my antenna is up."

"Glad to hear that you're on the alert. I'm comforted to know that."

"In other words, I gather that you've got nothing further to say on the matter."

"You gather correctly. But I appreciate the information."

"Just remember where it came from," Lon said.

"If I happen to forget, I am sure you'll remind me." I said, using a word I won't repeat and hanging up. I turned to Wolfe and repeated my conversation with Lon, along with a summary of the description I had given him earlier of Chester from my bridge game at McCready's. "He seemed like a decent sort," I continued, "although he did admit to being curious about the overall mood in that back room at the bar."

"Do you feel we would be imposing upon Saul to ask that he appear at McCready's again tonight, ready for bridge?" Wolfe asked.

"I don't. I assume you want him to act surprised about what happened to Chester Miller."

"Your assumption is accurate."

"I also assume you expect me to call him."

"Accurate again."

I dialed Saul and he answered after several rings as Wolfe picked up his instrument. "I don't know if you've heard, but one of your fellow bridge players was found dead in the Hudson."

"No, I hadn't. Who's the victim?"

"Chester Miller, and he had been shot in the head. We got the word from Lon Cohen."

"Has it been in the papers yet?"

"The police report came too late for the *Times* and the other morning papers, but according to Lon, it probably will make the

Gazette's first edition, which should be hitting our front steps any minute now."

"Saul, would you be able to go to McCready's tonight?" It was Wolfe, who had joined the conversation.

"Yes, sir. You'll want me to gauge the mood in there, right?"

"It would be helpful to get the benefit of your observations."

"I will drop in at McCready's and report back. Will you again be on your stool at the bar, Archie?"

I looked at Wolfe, who shook his head. "No, I'll take a pass tonight," I said. "But I plan to assess the mood—if there is one— in that flophouse across the street where I've been staying."

The *Gazette* had indeed arrived. Standing on the front porch, I leafed through it and found a two-paragraph item in the lower left-hand corner of page 28.

BODY FOUND IN HUDSON

The body identified, by papers on his person, as Chester Miller, 67, was discovered floating in the Hudson this morning by a passerby at Fifty-Eighth Street. The victim was wedged between pilings adjoining a Hudson River pier.

The police reported that Mr. Miller had been shot in the head and that the bullet had exited his skull. He was a retired employee of the U.S. Post Office and had been a mail carrier until his retirement three years ago.

I showed Wolfe the item without comment. "It would appear that being a bridge player in the back room at McCready's can be detrimental to one's health," he said, tossing the *Gazette* aside. Ever the wit.

* * *

That evening, I returned to my quarters in the Elmont, hoping to run into some of my fellow residents. On the way up the stairs to the fourth floor, I encountered an individual I had not seen before, a thin, almost emaciated man in middle age who wore his salt-and-pepper hair short and was dressed in clothes that seemed to be made for a larger person.

"Hello, my name is Art," I said with a grin, holding out a hand. "I don't believe I have seen you before."

The man didn't quite recoil, but he clearly was startled. He took my hand and made a feeble attempt at shaking it, then pulled away.

"Have you lived here long?" I asked, pressing the issue and forcing him to speak.

He looked like he wanted to run, but I was blocking the way down the stairs. "I . . . am new, very new," he said, pronouncing each word precisely, as if trying, without much success, to mask an accent. He was only partially successful, at least to my ears. Based on that short sentence, he might have been from almost anywhere in Europe. I pressed on.

"And your name is?" I asked, maintaining my grin.

"George."

"Where do you come from, George?"

"I am . . . how would you say it . . . a displaced person. I am from . . . Poland."

"It must have been very hard for you to get here."

"Very hard, yes," George said, clearly eager to end the conversation and get away from me.

"How many other displaced persons have come to New York?"

He shrugged, palms up. "I do not know," he answered, eager to squirm by me and head down the stairs.

"Well, I am glad you were able to make it here," I told him, stepping aside. He took the steps two at a time and did not look back.

CHAPTER 12

I allowed George—if that was his name—to get well away from me before I reversed course and went down to the lobby, then crossed Tenth Avenue to McCready's. I took one of the stools at the bar and ordered the usual scotch on the rocks, making no attempt to look in the direction of the back room. What I did see out of the corner of my eye, however, was that George, who I had just accosted in the stairwell of the Elmont, stood at the far end of the bar in what seemed to be a very private conversation with Liam McCready. And both of them were looking at me as they talked. Situations like that could give a guy a complex.

I ignored them, pretending to focus on the Dodgers game on television. After a few minutes, none other than McCready himself—without George—came up to me from behind the bar. "I do not believe I know you," he said with a smile, "but I have seen you in here a few times now, and I do like to get to know my customers. I am Liam McCready." He was husky without being fat, had red hair beginning to go gray, and with Ireland showing all over his ruddy face and evident in his speech.

"Nice to meet you," I said, shaking the freckled hand that had been offered. "I'm Art Horstmann."

"I am glad to see you, and also pleased that you have chosen to patronize our humble establishment. Do you reside in the neighborhood?"

"Yes, at least for now. I'm right across the street at the Elmont."

"By 'at least for now,' does that mean your stay there is to be of but a temporary nature?"

"I'm from out of town, a little burg in Ohio that no one has ever heard of, and I have come here looking for my cousin Ted, who seems to have disappeared."

"Really? And you have no idea what did happen to him?" the barkeeper asked, resting thick arms on the scarred mahogany surface of the bar.

"No idea whatever. Actually, you might have seen him there in your back room, playing bridge," I said, hoping he had not noticed me in that game one night myself.

"Ah, yes, the bridge players," McCready said, nodding. "They have always seemed to be indeed a pleasant bunch. So, he was one of them?"

"Yes, so I'm told. And while I am here, I'll be staying in his apartment right across the street." I had wondered if McCready might mention what had happened to Chester Miller. He didn't.

"I am surely sorry to hear about your cousin, Mr. Horstmann—or can I call you Art?"

"Sure, you can, I'm not the formal type. Seems like you have always got a lively crowd in here," I observed.

"At night, that is truly the case, but during the day it can get pretty slow in here. A lot of our customers are longshoremen from over on the docks," McCready said, jabbing a thumb in the direction of the Hudson. "But the minute their day shift is done, a good many of them head straight over here. I like to think of our little establishment as a haven where they can relax and enjoy themselves after putting in an honest day's work."

"Admirable," I said. "Have you run the bar for a long time?"

"Several years, it has been. I took it over after my uncle died. I am from Ireland, County Donegal."

"I never would have guessed it," I said, and we both laughed.

"They say an Irishman never loses his brogue, you know," McCready said, "and I suppose I would be a good example of that fine old adage. I gather that you started coming in here because of its propinquity to your current dwelling place."

"Propinquity—now that is quite a word," I told him, "one that you don't hear thrown around every day. I am impressed." Being around Wolfe for so long, I happened to know what the term meant, but I played dumb, which is not difficult for me.

"Aw, we Irish are always showing off our vocabularies," McCready said, pretending to be embarrassed. "I suppose 'tis part of our tradition as storytellers. Pay me no mind. Back on the subject of your cousin: Have you had any success in your search for him?"

"None whatever. It seems that Ted has vanished just like that," I replied, snapping my fingers. "And he has always been such a cautious person. I can't imagine what would have happened to him."

"It is strange, all right, Art. I will most certainly keep my eyes and ears open. Being behind the bar, where I find myself much of each day, I hear things—sometimes things I am probably not supposed to hear, if you read me." He rolled his eyes.

"I read you. But anything you happen to hear will be most welcome. Nobody across the street in the Elmont seemed to know my cousin. I find the residents over there to be a very strange bunch."

"Oh, and how might that be?" McCready asked, eyes wide.

"It seems like the ones who I've run into are very private, to the point of secrecy. By nature, I'm a friendly guy and I like to talk to people, but these new neighbors of mine, if I can call them that, don't want to talk at all."

"You said that you hail from Ohio, right?" the barkeep asked.

"I did."

"Well, I have not yet had the pleasure of visiting Ohio, but from what I have learned in my years in this fair land, people who come from areas away from the East Coast tend to be warmer and more open—like yourself, for instance. While New Yorkers, as I have had occasion to learn, are in general a suspicious lot and not given to making friends easily. Perhaps that is what you now are experiencing."

"Except my impression is that the people living in the Elmont—at least the ones I've met—are not New Yorkers. If anything, I would say they are not even native-born Americans."

"Really? And where do you think they might hail from?"

"I don't know, because those I've encountered in the halls and the stairways try to avoid speaking to me at all, and when they do, it seems like their grasp of English is somewhere between weak and nonexistent."

"Hmm. 'Tis something of a mystery, Art. Come to mention it, I have run across a fellow in here, maybe even two or three, who might live in the Elmont and who sound like they originated from somewhere in Europe, I am not sure of which countries. It could very well be that they are among those who are called displaced persons and who have earned the right to come to the United States. As I am sure you are aware, conditions in much of Europe continue to be difficult, even this many years after the end of that horrible war."

"Yes, I know the rebuilding of the countries over there has been slow, and we are taking in thousands who have nowhere else to go because they've lost their homes. Who can quarrel with the action that our country has undertaken?"

"Well said. It might also explain why some of your neighbors across the street are so cautious about talking to strangers. You and I can only begin to imagine what all of the displaced persons here have been through."

"Good point, I will keep that in mind. Well, it's time for me to get back to my home away from home," I said, putting money on the bar to cover my drink and a tip.

"I trust that you shall soon get news about your cousin," McCready said. "As I told you before, I will be alert as to anything concerning him. You said his name was Ted. . . ?"

"Yes, Ted Horstmann. I will likely be back in here." The owner nodded a good-bye as I walked out of his tavern, taking a quick look through the doorway at the back room, where the card table sat unoccupied. Once outside, I pondered on Liam McCready's use of the words "did happen to him" in relation to Theodore. Maybe it was simply his normal speech pattern, or perhaps McCready thought he knew what had already occurred, especially given the fate that had befallen another of the bridge players.

Back in apartment 412 at the Elmont, I took off my sports coat and also the shoulder holster, which I had begun wearing, along with my Marley .38. I was on a case some years ago up in the Bronx in which I left my weapon at home, and the lapse nearly cost me my life. I have never again made that mistake.

I wanted to telephone Saul at home, but there was no instrument in Theodore's room. The apartment house, if it can be so termed, could hardly afford its residents making calls to heaven knows where. I went downstairs and out, walking across the street and down to a Rexall drugstore on the corner, lit brightly like a beacon on the darkened block. The place was deserted except for a couple of teenagers on stools at the soda fountain making eyes at each other and slurping a chocolate milkshake through straws that went into the same Coca-Cola shaped glass. It could have been a frame out of an Andy Hardy film with Judy Garland and Mickey Rooney doing the guzzling and gazing at each other.

If I popped a balloon right behind them, I would not have broken their trance. The only other person in the shop was a white-jacketed soda jerk who pointedly avoided the loving couple as he straightened goods on shelves in an attempt to look busy.

I eased into the phone booth, closed the door, and popped a nickel into the slot, dialing a number I had memorized long ago. Saul answered after a couple of rings.

"Wasn't sure that I'd get you at home," I told him.

"As a matter of fact, I just walked in. I have had myself an interesting evening."

"So have I. Should we compare notes?"

"Sounds like a good idea," Saul said, "although I would prefer to do it face-to-face. Got any suggestions?"

"If you don't mind turning right around and going back outside again. There's a coffee shop about three blocks from what I'm referring to as my temporary residence. It's at Forty-Ninth and Eighth, far enough from both the Elmont and McCready's bar that we'd be unlikely to run into anyone from either of those establishments."

"I know the place, Archie. Give me twenty minutes to get there."

CHAPTER 13

In fact, it was eighteen minutes later that Saul came into the shop and spotted me in a booth at the back. "This cloak-and-dagger stuff is pretty exciting, isn't it?" he said out of the corner of his mouth as he slid in across from me.

"Yeah, a thrill a minute. Which of us gets to play Bogart?"

"That would be you. I'm more the George Raft type."

"In your dreams. Now tell me about this 'interesting evening' you've had."

"As planned, I went to McCready's on the off chance that one of the bridge players might show up, and damned if one did—Sid, that's Sid Meyer."

"I remember him, the retired barber. Seems like he's a nice fellow."

"Agreed. He had read about what happened to Chester, but said he came back to the bar because he was curious about the details and thought somebody might know something."

"Did he get there ahead of you?"

"No, I beat him by about five minutes. And when I stepped into the back room, I got these weird looks from the pool-playing longshoremen, as if I were a leper."

"Maybe they were hoping they had seen the last of the bridge players in what they consider their private preserve, so you likely were a disappointment," I said.

"Maybe. Anyway, I just looked around the room—what else was there to do?—when Sid walked in, wearing a dazed expression. I suggested to him that we go somewhere else to talk, anywhere else. He knew of another bar, a place about three blocks away, and he suggested calling Harvey, the other bridge player. He got hold of him at home, and the upshot was the three of us met in a quiet corner of a quiet saloon on Eleventh Avenue.

"It was like a wake. Those two guys and Chester had gotten really close over the years. They didn't just play bridge together, they also went as a group to baseball and basketball games."

"Did they have any ideas about what happened to Chester?"

"It was kind of hard getting them to talk because they were pretty broken up. I finally let the cat out of the bag, so to speak, and told them who I really was."

"An intrepid and tireless private investigator?"

"In so many words, smart guy."

"How did they react to that?"

"At first, I felt a little hostility, or at least strong reserve, from each of them. But then they softened when I told them how 'Ted' was someone I knew and was concerned about, and that I joined their bridge game to try to learn what might have befallen him. I did not, however, tell them who Theodore really was, or that he's in a hospital. They still seem to think he is missing."

"Fine to let them think so, even though it seems clear both of them probably figure it's likely that he is dead."

"I suppose so," Saul said, sipping on the cup of coffee that had just been set before him. "It's clear these two guys are scared, and who wouldn't be in their situation? One from their bridge foursome is killed, another has disappeared."

"I know these guys had been edgy around the longshoremen," I said. "Theodore had been quoted as saying they acted like they were 'up to no good,' whatever that means, and Chester also said they 'seemed to be hiding something.' It's all pretty vague."

Saul nodded. "I pressed Sid and Harvey, trying to get the pair to be specific about what made them uneasy about the patrons in McCready's, and neither one seems able to put a finger on specifically what made them nervous in that back room. The best I could get was when Harvey said, 'It was like they all'—he meant the pool players—'were hiding something, or had some sort of secret.'"

"Did either of them notice any kind of change in the makeup of the other customers at the bar?"

"I asked that," Saul said, "and they didn't seem aware of a shift, although Sid did mention that he thought a few of the people who sat at the bar had what he called 'a foreign feeling about them, not necessarily bad, just foreign.'"

"Similar to the residents I've been running into at the Elmont, that five-story pile of bricks I've been staying at across the street from McCready's."

"Some people get to have all the fun," Saul observed.

"Yeah, how'd you like to bunk there in my place? I'm willing to share the fun."

"No thanks. So, assuming there are more 'foreigners' both in that apartment building and McCready's salon, where are they coming from?"

"I may have at least a partial answer," I said, proceeding to tell Saul about what Charlie King from the North River docks told me about a group of men who had been seen getting off a National Export Lines freighter just in from Europe.

"It sounds like they could be displaced persons who, for whatever reasons, didn't qualify for residence here and are getting smuggled in," Saul said. "And maybe that's also the explanation for all those others in the Elmont and at McCready's."

"Okay, I will give you that. But how does it explain the violence against Theodore and the murder of Chester Miller, both events which seem to be related to the secretive nature in McCready's and possibly at the Elmont as well? If anything, you would think these DPs who get smuggled in would try above all to avoid attention."

"Good point," Saul said. "What if it's not the DPs who are behind the violence?"

"You're suggesting the longshoremen?"

"I am not sure what I'm suggesting. But if I were you, I would watch my back while you're staying at the Elmont and hanging around that saloon. Things are going on that we don't fully understand."

"I will keep that advice in mind," I told him. And as it turned out, it was a good thing I did.

CHAPTER 14

After leaving Saul, I went back to the Elmont and turned in, wedging a chair under the knob of my door to the hall as a precaution against prowlers, something I should have done earlier. I'm a sound sleeper, and especially after my discussion with Saul, I began to feel somewhat paranoid.

The next morning, I returned to the coffee shop down the street for ham, eggs, and hash browns, resisting the temptation to show up at the brownstone for some of Fritz's first-rate breakfast fare. At the crowded counter as I was polishing off my second cup of coffee, I considered my options. I could either go back to the Elmont and try to draw out some of my fellow roomers or go poke around the National Export docks to see if any more "passengers" were debarking from the company's ships. I didn't like either option, so I headed for the brownstone, where I could make myself useful by catching up on Wolfe's correspondence.

I hit the buzzer with my usual combination of long-and-short buzzes, and Fritz pulled the door open with what I took to be a relieved smile. "I worry about you when you are not here, Archie," he said.

"I appreciate that. Have you heard anything about Theodore?"

"Dr. Vollmer telephoned yesterday afternoon and told Mr. Wolfe that his condition has not changed. The doctor said he was neither surprised nor discouraged."

"Is anything else happening around here?"

"I do not think Mr. Wolfe is pleased with his new gardener, Mr. Willis. It has made him more difficult than usual in the kitchen. I cannot seem to please him. We had a fight last night over whether to use shallots in baked scallops. I have done it the same way for years and have never had any complaints, and now he is unhappy with me."

"Your lot is not an easy one," I told him. "But it's been that way for years, isn't that true?"

Fritz nodded, his expression woeful. "I work very hard to please him, Archie."

"I know you do. And if I am allowed to have a vote in this discussion, I think you are a marvel in the kitchen, and always have been."

He mumbled a thank-you and turned back to the kitchen, while I went into the office. Fritz had neatly stacked the morning mail on my desk. I slit all the envelopes and pulled out the only bill to be paid, from Murger's, where Wolfe buys his books. On my desk were several letters I had previously typed, signed by Wolfe and ready to be mailed. I set to work.

I had finished my chores when the boss came down from the plant rooms after his morning session with the orchids. He settled in at his desk, rang for beer, asked if I had slept well, and gave me a look that indicated I should report.

"Yes, I slept well, although I would rather have been in my own room upstairs. I understand Vollmer called and told Fritz there has been no change in Theodore's condition."

"Yes, although the doctor remains optimistic. What have you learned since last we spoke?"

"Not a lot." I filled Wolfe in on my conversation with Liam McCready and Saul's meeting with Sid and Harvey. "We are both stumped about what's really going on in what I'm going to call the 'Mysterious Triangle'—the National Export dock, McCready's saloon, and the Elmont. It seems clear that people are getting smuggled into the country. I'm sure it's because more people want to come here than the law allows."

"That is patently true," Wolfe said. "President Truman's Displaced Person's Act of 1948 allowed for the admission of two hundred thousand immigrants over a two-year period. Recently, that number has been raised to four hundred thousand, but I have read in the newspapers that far greater numbers continue to seek asylum here."

"Well, I have to assume that somebody is making big money by sneaking others in."

"A valid assumption. And it seems apparent the amount of money changing hands is significant enough that violence is being done to those who have suspicions of impropriety and illegality."

"There ought to be a special place in hell for those who get rich on the suffering of others," I put in.

"As Sophocles wrote more than twenty-four centuries ago, 'For money, you would sell your soul,'" Wolfe said. "Countless souls have ransomed themselves over the centuries for profit."

"I suppose so. Have you got any thoughts on how we should now proceed?"

"I believe your stay at that apartment building is nearing

its completion. It appears you have mined that lode for all of the ore you are likely to get. Those card players Saul spoke to, Sid and Harvey. Do you feel we might benefit if I were to talk to them?" Only on rare occasions has Wolfe asked my advice, which usually means he is at least temporarily stymied.

"A good question. In the past, I've interviewed countless people, thinking that I milked them dry. And then they come in here, and within a half hour, often less, you have been able to find out far more than I did twice the time."

Wolfe leaned back in his chair and sighed. "Based on what you have said, Saul knows the two gentlemen better than you do."

"There's no question whatever. He has spent more time with them than I have, both at the bridge table and in conversation, including their recent session away from McCready's."

"That being the case, I suggest Saul persuade them to come here, and we already know his powers of persuasion are considerable. He will of course need to reveal our identities and that of Theodore as well."

"I'll give him a call. Do you want to be on the line?"

"Not necessary," Wolfe said, browsing an orchid catalog that arrived in the morning mail.

I got Saul at home and relayed Wolfe's request. "So, I spill the beans about you guys and Theodore as well, right?" he asked.

"Do you see that as a problem?"

"Oh . . . not really, Archie. I'm sure they'll be surprised at first, but when I tell them Nero Wolfe is seeking not just the people who beat Horstmann half to death but those who killed Chester as well, I think that ought to seal the deal. When does he want to see them?"

I turned to Wolfe, holding up the receiver so he could he part of the conversation, whether he wanted to or not. "Assuming Saul can get the pair to come, did you have a time in mind?"

"Would he be able to deliver them here tonight at nine?"

"I will give it a try," Saul said. "You'll hear from me sometime this afternoon, one way or the other."

In fact, Saul got back to me just after 4 p.m., which meant, of course, that Wolfe was up in the plant rooms for his afternoon session. "I will bring them both at nine," he said. "And in answer to the question you are about to ask, they were surprised, make that *very* surprised, to learn about you and Wolfe, and of course about Theodore."

"Were they angry or upset?"

"Not either, really. Once they got over the initial shock, I think they both were encouraged. And they were particularly pleased to learn their friend 'Ted' was alive. Although I didn't sugarcoat his condition in the least."

"We'll be ready for all of you at nine," I told him, hanging up and then calling Wolfe in the plant rooms.

"Yes!" he barked. The man has never learned telephone etiquette and never will. And it didn't help that he hates to be disturbed when he's playing with his "concubines," as he refers to the orchids that fill and glorify those three rooms in the greenhouse on the roof.

When I told him of Saul's success, he did manage to mutter a "satisfactory" before slamming down his instrument.

CHAPTER 15

At 8:45 p.m., the doorbell rang and I did the honors. On the stoop were Saul with the men I recognized as Sid and Harvey, although their garb was different from when I played bridge with them. Both sported jackets and ties, perhaps because they felt a meeting with Nero Wolfe demanded a certain amount of decorum.

"Please come in," I said, and I got looks of uncertainty from each of our guests. "I assume you both now know that I am not 'Art,' but rather Archie Goodwin, assistant to Nero Wolfe."

"We do," said an unsmiling Harvey, who eyed me over his ever-present half-glasses. Sid nodded but said nothing.

When we got to the office, I gestured the two to yellow chairs facing Wolfe's desk, while Saul slid into the red leather chair normally reserved for a client or Cramer. "Can I get anyone a drink? We have a well-stocked bar," I said, nodding to the table against the wall.

"I'll have a scotch and water," Saul said, breaking the ice, so to speak.

"Make that two," said Sid.

"Do you have rye? If so, I would like it on the rocks," put in Harvey.

I nodded, playing bartender for the trio. Our visitors did not seem surprised that Wolfe wasn't present, which meant Saul had told them of their host's habit of not appearing until his audience was seated.

After everyone had their drinks, Wolfe strode in, as if on cue. He nodded, settled behind the desk, and rang for beer. "Gentlemen, thank you for accepting our invitation. I realize both Mr. Goodwin and Mr. Panzer were, by intent, not forthcoming about their identities when you first encountered them at the bridge table in McCready's. Before I begin talking, I invite each of you to ask as many questions as you wish to any of the three of us. I promise candor in our responses."

Sid and Harvey looked at each other, and Sid began. "Needless to say, sir, we were surprised when Saul told us who he was and who Art—make that Archie—was. And we knew nothing about Ted's real background until we also learned that from Saul. It has taken us awhile to digest all of this." Harvey nodded his agreement.

"Your reactions are understandable," Wolfe said as he took a drink from the first of two chilled beers Fritz had brought in. "And you now are aware that Theodore Horstmann, the man you know as Ted, is in my employ and currently lies in a coma at a local hospital."

It was Harvey's turn to speak. "Yes, and we also learned from Saul that he was viciously beaten. What is his prognosis?"

"It is uncertain," Wolfe replied. "Both Theodore and your friend Chester were attacked, Chester fatally. Do either of you have any thoughts as to why these two were targeted. And by whom?"

"Chester was the gentlest of men, and although I can't speak for Ted, he also seemed to be the nonviolent type," Harvey said, turning to Sid. "What do you think?"

"Each of them seemed to be very bothered by the people around them at McCready's. Or maybe suspicious is a more accurate word," Sid said.

"What fueled their suspicion?" Wolfe asked.

"I am not sure about Ted's reasons," Sid said, "being that he has been very tight-lipped—friendly, but tight-lipped. Another thing about Ted: Whenever German was spoken by the DPs sitting at the bar, I got the feeling he could understand them.

"As for Chester, he has always been the most perceptive and sensitive of the three of us. And almost since we began playing bridge in that back room at McCready's, he was the one who seemed to be the most attuned to his surroundings."

"Be specific."

Sid took a deep breath and closed his eyes. "Chester was suspicious of the pool players. Now longshoremen can be rough customers to begin with, but he saw them, or at least some of them, as more than that. He told Harvey and me that he felt that these guys were acting suspicious. Oh, sure, they were derisive to us and thought that we were playing a ladies' game, but that wasn't what bothered Chester. He said they acted like they had something to hide."

"Did he express any thoughts as to what that 'something' might be?"

"I can answer that," Harvey said. "Chester told me one night that he figured it had something to do with displaced persons, or DPs, as they are called, and Sid here agreed with him."

"What made him think that?" Wolfe asked.

"He—and the rest of us, for that matter—had begun to notice a shift in the type of people who came into McCready's. There were still plenty of dockworkers, all right, but there also was a new group who seemed to be foreign from my perspective. They did not talk much in the bar, at least not out loud, although they did mutter very quietly to one another. And they definitely liked their beer."

Wolfe dabbed his lips with a handkerchief. "How many were in this new group?"

It was Sid's turn to respond. "At any one time, maybe about a half-dozen or so. But it wasn't always the same half-dozen. They seemed to drift in and out."

"To what degree did they interact with the longshoremen?"

"Hardly at all. If anything, the two groups seemed to ignore each other," Sid replied.

"Back to the longshoremen. Do either of you know if they were employed at a specific dock?"

"I do, because I heard a couple of them talking in the back room while they were playing pool," Harvey answered. "They were complaining and loudly, about their working conditions, and one of them said, 'That's typical of the type of straw bosses they hire at that damned National Export Lines. They act like prison guards the way they bark orders and strut.' That got the other pool players nodding in agreement and adding to the grumbling. It seemed like all of them were working for National Export."

"Do either of you see any reason why someone would have targeted Chester—or Theodore, for that matter?" Wolfe asked.

"For one thing, Chester seemed to be more conscious of the presence of the pool players than Sid or me," Harvey said. "We both tried to ignore them and their conversations. But Chester was always looking over at the group. And on at least two occasions that I can recall, he made some snide remarks to Ted about them—remarks the longshoremen easily would have heard, and did, because they sent some dirty looks in our direction."

"What makes you think that longshoremen were behind what befell both men?"

"I wouldn't want to say that for sure," Harvey answered, "but I can tell you this much: I am not setting foot in that saloon again—ever!"

"Same here," Sid echoed.

Wolfe leaned back and drew in a bushel of air. "Do either of you know any displaced persons?"

Harvey shook his head but Sid jumped in. "I do, a second cousin, Hyman, and his wife. They're from Holland and they fled the Germans, but they were thrown into prison like so many other Jews. Fortunately, they were able to survive until the Allies liberated them, although they weren't treated very well by the Germans, and they still aren't what I would call fully healthy.

"They came over here last year on that DP act of the president's and are living over in Brooklyn now in a small flat," Sid continued. "They are struggling but surviving, and those of us related to them have pitched in one way or another to give whatever help we can. It's the very least we can do. Another cousin of mine was able to find Hyman a job in a kosher restaurant. He had been a cook—or as he likes to put it, a 'chef'—in Amsterdam before the war."

"Millions of people have suffered greatly," observed Wolfe, who himself was sending funds regularly to relatives of his own in Montenegro and other Balkan states. "The world is still far from recovering from the ravages of the war." He turned to Sid and Harvey. "Gentlemen, do you have any other observations that might help us as we investigate the attacks on Chester and Theodore—the man you have referred to as Ted?"

They both shook their heads, and Harvey said, "Please continue to let us know about Ted's condition."

"We will," Saul said. "I will make a point of keeping you both updated, with Mr. Wolfe's approval, of course."

Wolfe nodded but said nothing. He rose, walking out of the office without a backward look.

"I hope we didn't say something to insult him," Sid remarked.

"Oh no, not at all," I reassured our visitors, both of whom seemed understandably puzzled by their host's abrupt departure. "He wasn't being rude, that is just his manner. Brevity is his middle name."

"Well, we really should be going," Harvey said. "Thank you for your hospitality."

"We may want to reach you again," I told them.

"I have their phone numbers," Saul said. There were handshakes all around, and we saw the two subdued men to the front door. After they had gone, Saul and I stayed in the office for a time, nursing our drinks and playing gin rummy. It is not necessary to discuss the outcome of the game.

CHAPTER 16

The next morning after an eight-hour sleep in my bedroom at the brownstone and Fritz's breakfast of Canadian bacon, an apricot omelet, and blueberry muffins, I sat at my desk in the office getting caught up on correspondence and entering orchid germination records on file cards from notes Carl Willis had brought down.

I had just finished going through the morning mail when the phone rang. It was Doc Vollmer. "I am calling to report there has been no change in Theodore Horstmann's condition," he said.

"Would you call that good or bad news?"

"Neither," he sniffed. "On the plus side, his vital signs remain strong. On the minus side, he shows no indication of emerging from the coma."

"Is there anything that can be done to somehow awaken him?"

"There is not," Vollmer said, his tone clearly indicating that he was appalled by my lack of medical knowledge.

"I will pass your report along to Mr. Wolfe," I told the doctor in an icy tone of my own.

I gave Wolfe Vollmer's report when he came down from the plant rooms at eleven. He made no comment, ringing for beer.

"I still have some of my gear in Theodore's room at the Elmont," I told him. "Should I pack it up and come home for good, as you have suggested?"

"I would prefer that you stay there one more night," Wolfe said. "It is possible you will still be able to learn something."

When Wolfe says he would "prefer" me to do something, what he really means, is *You shall do this*. I don't know what he expected me to find out by staying yet another day, although I suspect that, as sometimes happens, he is currently at a dead end and is giving me something to do to show that he's working. I was of course damned unhappy having to spend yet another night in that tired old building on Tenth Avenue, but I also long ago had gotten used to going along with orders from the man who signs my paychecks.

But lest you get the idea that I am afraid of going it alone without Wolfe out in the big, bad world, I am my own man and can quit at any time, as I have threatened in the past. In fact, on two occasions, Saul Panzer and I have discussed, if only in the vaguest of terms, starting our own detective agency.

If I am being totally honest with myself, however, one of the factors keeping me in Wolfe's employ is that were I to leave, I would be depriving myself of Fritz Brenner's superb meals. Does that make me weak-willed? I leave it to you to decide. Speaking of Fritz's cuisine, I delayed going back to my home away from home until after I had feasted on one of his specialties: Cape Cod clam cakes, served with a sour sauce.

After lunch, I still wasn't ready to go back to Tenth Avenue, so I found ways to busy myself by shining two pairs of shoes and dusting my room. When I finally and reluctantly left, Wolfe had already gone up for his two-hour afternoon session with the orchids.

As I entered the Elmont's tired lobby on that rainy late afternoon, I ran into the building's super, Erwin Bauer. "Ah, Mr. . . . Horstmann, isn't it?" he said. "Have you had any success in locating your uncle?"

"Not so far. I will be going back home to Ohio, but I do plan on coming back and keeping 412, at least for a while. Do I owe you any rent?"

"No, as I said before, you are all paid up through next month. Do you think that you will be returning soon?"

"I don't know. Are you concerned that someone else will want the apartment?"

"Oh, no, no, if I have your promise that you will be here again before the end of next month," Bauer said, rubbing the stubble on his chin as if deep in thought, which in his case seemed highly improbable.

"You have my promise, Mr. Bauer. Are all of your apartments occupied right now?"

He did that chin rub again. "Well . . . we have a very high demand because of our excellent location."

"Pardon my ignorance as an out-of-towner, but what is it that makes this an excellent location? I ask only because as a visitor I don't know New York City all that well."

He looked at me through narrowed eyes. "I figure you've stayed here long enough to see that for yourself. Look, we're on a busy street with lots of taxis, close to subway stations, and there are shops and restaurants all over the place," he said with the sweep of an outstretched arm as if to encompass the whole of Hell's Kitchen.

"Good point. Maybe that's why my uncle Ted chose the place. How long have you been the Elmont's superintendent?"

I could see that Bauer was getting uneasy. "I've been here for, let's see . . . oh, about seven years now. Sorry, but I have to check the furnace room," he said, doing an about-face and opening a door which I assume led to the furnaces. With an outside temperature of more than seventy degrees, I had to wonder why the building's heating system needed checking.

I went upstairs to 412 and packed the few clothes I had hung in the closet and had put in the drawer of a chest. One more night here. Actually, it wasn't all that bad, but, compared with my room in the brownstone . . .

I briefly contemplated a trip across the street to McCready's saloon but vetoed the idea; it was too early to start ingesting anything alcoholic. I seldom take a drink before sunset, and even though the downpour had darkened the sky early for this time of year, I felt that didn't allow me to alter my principles. Besides, I had not been getting enough exercise lately, so a long walk was in order. Before I had gotten more than a few blocks, however, the rain was back, so I ducked into a steak house and decided on an early dinner. The filet I ordered was decent, although I had enjoyed far better ones in the brownstone—no surprise there.

By the time I walked outside, the rain had stopped, but the clouds hadn't cleared, so it was unnaturally dark on what was one of the longest days of the year. I risked a stroll without an umbrella, enjoying one of those refreshing times following a rain that cleanse the air. There was almost no pedestrian traffic, perhaps because people expected more rain. With no destination in mind, I headed south on Tenth Avenue. After going a little more than a block, I sensed I had acquired a shadow.

As one who has done a good bit of tailing myself, I am sensitive to pedestrian traffic, and, without turning to look behind me, I was all but positive I was being followed. I stopped to glance into the window of an Automat, as if watching customers dine on plain food at plain tables, and out of the corner of my eye I saw a silhouette freeze and press against the wall of a building some fifty yards behind me. I stepped up my pace and turned west into a side street that ran toward the Hudson.

Halfway down the block, I eased into the recessed doorway of an automobile garage that looked to be closed. After what seemed like a minute but probably was less, I heard footfalls that made squishy sounds because of puddles in the sidewalk.

The sounds grew louder as I pushed back into the alcove. A figure holding what appeared to be a yard-long metal bar passed within a foot of me but never turned in my direction. I silently stepped out behind him and put a hammerlock on his right arm, the one holding the bar, which clanked onto the sidewalk. He groaned as his knees buckled and he spit out words I didn't understand.

"All right, what gives with the tail?" I barked in his ear as I kept the pressure on that arm. "Talk, dammit!"

While I waited for an answer from this guy and thought about what a lousy shadower he made, there was a noise behind me. It was the last thing I heard.

The pain was the worst in my head. Or was it the worst in my shoulders, which were being stretched? I had trouble breathing, too. I got dragged along with my feet feeling like they had lead weights strapped on. I wanted to go to sleep but couldn't seem to talk to whoever or whatever was making me move forward. I finally got the idea that someone was on either side of me, hands under my armpits, with the one on my right smelling like sauerkraut.

"Hey . . . hey," I think I said, getting a slap on the side of my head from Sauerkraut Breath. I tried getting out of his grip, but I got another slap for my effort, this one harder. Next, I tried going limp, which wasn't hard, because my legs were like rubber. That worked a little better, because I got dropped onto the sidewalk as my "escorts" made guttural mocking sounds. I groaned and rolled over on my side, slowly remembering I was not alone—the Marley .38 nestled snugly in the shoulder holster inside my sports coat.

I lay on the concrete, trying to buy time, and I got kicked in the legs for my trouble. I groaned again, this time partly for effect, and I got up slowly. These guys might be tough, but they were amateurs who apparently never thought to frisk me while I was out.

I rose to a knee as they stood over me, preparing to strike, and I slipped my hand inside my jacket. One of the pair suddenly realized what was happening, but he was a beat too slow. I have never considered myself particularly quick on the draw, but I was fast enough for these two, who found themselves suddenly gaping at the business end of a roscoe in a surprisingly steady hand. One of them lunged at me, and I hit him on the head with the butt of the Marley, sending him backward as I turned the gun on his partner, who tried to grab it from my hand.

As we struggled, the one I had coshed threw his shoulder against me and knocked me down, but I managed to get to my feet as they ran down the deserted street. I fired once, aiming at their legs, and I knew I had made a hit when I heard a scream from one of them, who began limping as his partner put an arm around him and tugged him along. I was in no condition to chase after them, though, as whatever adrenaline that had kicked in during the fray rapidly deserted me, to be replaced by stabbing pain in several places.

I was limping, myself, as I headed back to Tenth Avenue and the Elmont. The rain had started again, but I barely felt it with all of my other aches and also my chagrin. Years ago, when I was new to the detective trade, if our work can be termed a trade, Saul Panzer gave me several pieces of advice. One of them was this: "If someone is following you and you're able to catch him in the act, don't let down your guard, because there's a good chance that he has a 'trailer.'"

My trailer had hit me on the noggin with something hard enough that a ringing sound seemed to be bouncing around in my head, using it as a pinball machine. I didn't run into anyone as I entered the Elmont and stumbled up to the fourth floor, where I grabbed the bag containing my clothes and said good-bye to the place that had been, for, thankfully, a brief time, my second home.

On my way out the door of 412 for the last time, I paused in front of a mirror and did not like what I saw: My face was bruised in about three places, and my left cheek was the color of one of the fresh eggplants Fritz brings home from the market.

CHAPTER 17

I normally would have hoofed it back to the brownstone, but I was feeling none too steady on my pins, not to mention my head and other parts of my frame, so I flagged a Yellow and slumped into its back seat. At this time of day, the drive is a short one, usually ten minutes, fifteen tops, but the cabbie had to wake me when we got to Thirty-Fifth Street.

"C'mon, Mac, you're home. Go inside and sleep it off, you'll feel better in the morning. I know that only too well; I've been in that shape more times than I can count."

I tried to tell him that I was as sober as a Puritan judge at a New England witch trial, but it would have taken more effort than I cared to expend. I paid him and lumbered up the steps, leaning on the bell and pressing it with the longs-and-shorts code that Fritz knew.

"Archie! What has happened to you?" our world-class chef gasped as I staggered in, dropping my small suitcase on the floor. "Come into the front room and sit down," he said, leading me gently by an arm. "I will get Mr. Wolfe."

I tried to tell him not to bother, but he was gone. After what seemed like five minutes later but probably was far less, Wolfe stepped in with a stein of beer in one hand and looked down, considering me in my sprawl on the sofa.

"What has happened?" he barked.

"Not so loud!" I said, putting my palms over my ears. "There is no need to shout."

"I was not—" Wolfe cut himself off, realizing my condition. He lowered himself into the facing easy chair, one of several in the brownstone big enough to accommodate his girth. "Report, if you are able."

"You are damned right I'm able," I told him and then went into what must have been a rambling account of my evening's escapades. Wolfe sat, lips pursed, and took a drink. "I am going to telephone Dr. Vollmer," he declared, rising.

"No, I don't need—"

"Archie, be quiet!" he barked, walking back across the hall to the office. I worked myself into a sitting position, which wasn't easy, and leaned back, staring at the ceiling. "Archie, here is some tea, it will be refreshing," Fritz said, concern lining his face.

"You know I don't like tea!" I shot back, pushing the cup away and causing Fritz to recoil as if having been slapped. Wolfe reentered the front room and announced that "The doctor is on his way."

Before I could respond, Vollmer came in, panting. "Well, well," he shook his head and clucked in a tone they probably teach in medical school. "It seems that you have run into some trouble."

"Trouble ran into me," I replied, "but I'm fine. I just need a little rest."

"I will be the judge of that," the doctor said, pulling out his stethoscope. "Take off your tie and unbutton your shirt," he demanded in what I knew to be his standard bedside manner. "Um-hmm, yes, yes," he said, nodding to no one in particular and he moved the scope around on my chest. Next came a miniature flashlight, with which Vollmer peered into one of my eyes and then the other one, nodding again. "How are you feeling, Archie?"

"I feel fine, and as I just told you, Doc, a good night's sleep will do wonders for me."

"It will take more than just a good night's sleep," the sawbones remarked dryly. He took a rubber mallet out of his bag and tapped my knee, shaking his head. "What do you remember about tonight?" he asked.

"Too much," I said.

"Come, come, tell me exactly what happened," he insisted, running his fingers over my scalp, which I did not like one damned bit. Before I could relate the day's events, Vollmer said, "You've got a nasty cut right there. I'm surprised it didn't bleed much, but you're going to need stitches."

"You're full of good news, aren't you?"

"And I've got more of it," the doctor said. "All the signs are that you've got a concussion and will have to take it easy for a while."

"And just what does 'for a while' mean?"

"Seven to ten days, during which time you should stay inside, relax—if you even know how—and eat well and drink plenty of water. Oh, and I'm going to be suturing that gash in your head, which should take about three or maybe four stitches."

"Swell. Where do I have to go for you to do that."

"Archie, because you and Nero Wolfe are longtime patients as well as neighbors, I am perfectly willing to sew you up down the street in my office—right now. I believe your condition is such that you can walk that far."

I grumbled and started to stand, but got dizzy and plopped back down on the sofa. At that moment, Wolfe returned yet again to the front room, his expression one that demanded answers.

"It's a concussion," Vollmer told him. "I have already told Archie he needs to rest for more than a week. He can eat all he wants and should drink plenty of water. But no physical exertion whatever. Also, he's got a dandy slice on the head."

"Which you will attend to," Wolfe said.

"Yes, at my office, where we are going immediately. I'm going to call my nurse at home, if I may use your telephone."

With old Vollmer, of all people, supporting me although I felt I didn't need it, we made it to his establishment a few doors from the brownstone. It was never a place I cared to be, with one exception: Caroline.

She was the doctor's nurse and factotum, performing myriad duties in this medical workplace. More than that, she was shapely and lovely and had a warmth and cheerfulness that went a long way toward partially offsetting Vollmer's dour manner.

The doctor got me settled on a mini-operating table in his office and draped a sheet over my shoulders. We had been in the office for a few minutes before Caroline rushed in, breathless. "Mr. Goodwin, it is always so nice to see you," she said with a smile worthy of a toothpaste advertisement, "even when you are here on a less-than-pleasant matter. I am happy to tell you that from what the doctor has said to me on the phone, this process will be simple and brief."

"I know it will go well, if only you promise to hold my hand the entire time," I said.

"You know, Mr. Goodwin, that I would be more than happy to comply with your wishes, except that I fear the doctor will need me, including both of my hands, during the entire procedure," she said. "But I will be right beside you the entire time."

"Be still my heart," I told her as Vollmer, white coat and all, entered, casting a pall over the scene. I knew him to be a first-rate doctor, but he must have flunked *Bedside Manner 101* in medical school.

Anyway, Caroline was correct in her assessment. The procedure was brief and relatively painless, although I left with a portion of my hair shaved off and a rather large white dressing serving as my crown.

As I entered the brownstone, Fritz looked me over and, to his credit, he neither laughed nor stared. He was, he told me earnestly, happy that I was feeling better. Wolfe, who was at his desk reading, looked up, his eyes asking how I felt.

"Vollmer stitched me up, although he's made me look like a freak," I said.

I had more than nine hours of sleep that night, followed by an unusually late breakfast in the kitchen as Fritz fussed over me like a mother hen. Then I went to the office with coffee and flipped through the morning mail delivery, which held nothing of interest.

Wolfe came down from the plant rooms promptly at eleven and peered at me. "Good morning, Archie. How do you feel?" he asked as he placed an orchid raceme in the small vase on his desk, as was his daily practice.

"Well, as you can see, I look like I got into a snowball fight and one of the snowballs is still on my head. But otherwise, I'm upright and more or less fit."

"I realize from what the doctor has said that the next week or more will be a time of rest for you," Wolfe said, "so I hesitate to give you assignments."

"Hey, I am supposed to take it easy, not take to my bed. I'm not an invalid."

"Understood," he said. "Do you feel confident that when you fired at those men last night, you hit one of them?"

"Positive. As I said, I aimed low because I wasn't trying to kill anybody, but after what had happened to me, I wasn't above inflicting some pain and catching at least one of the pair. Obviously, I was no condition to catch anyone, but I did get one of them, either on an ankle or low down on a leg."

"As far as you were able to tell, were there any onlookers, eyewitnesses?"

"I don't think so. That section of street was deserted at the time."

"It is possible, but not likely, that the man went to an emergency room."

"I agree with your 'not likely.' As we both know, whenever someone with a gunshot wound goes to a hospital, reports have to be filled out and the police get involved. Those guys, whoever they were, would have avoided that."

"I will be placing an advertisement in the *Gazette*," he said.

"I'm ready," I told him, poising a pen over my note pad.

"The notice should be two columns wide, boxed, with an eighteen-point boldface headline reading **Witness Sought**. The body type will read: Wanted: any witnesses to a gunshot fired at an individual Wednesday night in the vicinity of Eleventh Avenue and . . ." He turned to me with an eyebrow raised.

"Fifty-Sixth Street," I said and wrote the words down.

Wolfe continued: "A reward will be given to anyone who provides substantive information."

"Anything else?"

"I know the newspaper then provides a box number at the bottom for those responding. At least that has been the case in the past."

"Right. I will call and set it up. You know, of course, that we will almost surely get reaction from our old friend, Mr. Cohen. He is used to you placing this type of ad."

"We shall be prepared for a response from Mr. Cohen. Let us hope it is not the only response we get."

CHAPTER 18

I dictated the text over the telephone and learned I was early enough that it would make it into the biggest editions of the *Gazette*, an afternoon paper. That made it possible we could get responses as early as tomorrow, although I had to wonder whether anyone had heard my gunshot on that deserted street near the Hudson.

I still felt the effects of my adventures the night before. My shoulders ached from the dragging I got, and I had a headache, although at least a part of that was likely from Doc Vollmer's stitches. But overall, I felt better than I had any right to.

After lunch, I went up to my room and lay down, trying to follow doctor's orders. To my surprise, I fell asleep, something I never do during the day. When I awoke and went down to my office, I found a note from Fritz on my desk: *Mr. Cohen called. He seemed agitated.* No surprise there.

I dialed Lon's number at the paper and got him on the second ring. "Cohen here."

"And Goodwin at this end. I understand you called."

"And just why do you suppose that would be?" he growled.

"I'm all ears," I said.

"I just bet you are. What ever happened to the spirit of cooperation?"

"Heck, I'm about as cooperative a guy as you're ever likely to find. I'm known as 'Mr. Cooperation.'"

"I don't think so," Lon replied, spacing his words for emphasis. "Let's talk about a certain item that was placed in today's editions. And don't try playing dumb with me. I know damned well that when I see a box like this in our pages, Nero Wolfe is almost always behind it."

"I do not have a comment at the present time."

"You sound like a Mafia boss on trial."

"I am cut to the quick, newshawk."

"Yeah, right. Was there some gunplay over in Hell's Kitchen?"

"That is what Mr. Wolfe and I have reason to believe."

"Uh-huh. Interesting that you have so much interest in that particular area, including that Tenth Avenue apartment building, the nearby saloon, and the North River docks, all places that you have asked us to look into. By the way, we have done some poking around and have come up empty."

"I appreciate the effort."

"Well thanks at least for that," Lon said. "You know of course that because of the item Wolfe is running in tonight's paper, we have no choice but to follow up on it. I've got a man over in Hell's Kitchen right now, poking around."

"I would expect nothing less from America's fifth-largest newspaper."

"Don't try buttering me up—it's too late for that. By the way, since this all started with your man Horstmann getting mugged, how is he doing?"

"Stable condition, still in a coma."

"Anything else you would like to tell me?"

"Not at the moment."

"All right then, what about some information sharing? As in: I'll tell you what our man over on the West Side learns about that shooting and you tell us about what kind of response your ad has gotten?"

"I will discuss that with Mr. Wolfe."

"Of course, you will. You're holding your cards pretty close to the vest, aren't you? A shame you don't play poker as well as you talk."

"Hey, I was the big winner last week, wasn't I?"

"For a change. But how could you possibly have lost with the cards that came your way? Even an orangutan could have taken home money with the hands you got dealt. Hell, three aces right off the bat. And then you drew a pair of fours giving you a full boat. The fates were smiling on you."

"Do I detect just the tiniest bit of jealousy emerging?"

"Nah, because next time I will win everything I lost to you, count on it. Get back to me after you've talked to Wolfe. So far, the *Gazette* has gotten shortchanged on this business."

"You know what my boss always tells you. When we get something, you'll be the first to know."

"Talk is cheap. Gotta run, we're up against a deadline, something you never have to worry about." I started to respond, but the line had gone dead. When Wolfe came down from the plant rooms at six, I told him about Lon's call.

"His reaction was to be expected, of course," he said as he rang for beer. "It is possible his people may learn something that may be of assistance to us."

"Yeah, but right now our Mr. Cohen is not in a mood to share anything with us. He thinks—" I was interrupted by the doorbell. I walked down the hall and saw the solid silhouette of Inspector Cramer through the one-way glass. When I told Wolfe, he said, "Get Fritz to answer the door. You can watch from the peephole."

"But I—"

"Go. I don't for the moment want him to see you in your condition. It gives rise to questions we are not now prepared to answer."

Regarding the "peephole" that Wolfe referred to, in the hall between the office and the kitchen, there is a small alcove inside of which one can secretly observe the office. It works like this: On the wall to the left of Wolfe and also to my left as I sit—there is a painting on glass of the Washington Monument. The painting is actually transparent and well-camouflaged, and it allows someone in the alcove to both view the office and hear any conversation. As Wolfe and I are within a half-inch of the same height, the peephole is designed to be at our eye level. We each have used it numerous times over the years.

I got to the peephole in time to see Cramer storm into the office carrying a rolled-up newspaper and an unlit cigar. He dropped into the red leather chair as is his habit and started using his cigar as a pointer, jabbing it at Wolfe. "Okay, just what gives with this ad?" he growled as he thrust the *Gazette* in Wolfe's direction.

"I beg your pardon," Wolfe responded, doing his best to appear puzzled.

"Don't get cute with me. You have run stuff like this before. It's become almost a trademark of yours."

"I did not realize I had become so predictable, Inspector."

"Hah! I can read you like a book, don't think I can't," he said, looking around the room and frowning. "By the way, where's Goodwin?"

"Archie is out at the moment. It may surprise you, but he does not always keep me apprised of his activities."

"Back to the ad. What's the story here? Is it somehow tied to what happened to Horstmann?"

Wolfe drew in air and exhaled slowly. "You cannot be positive I placed the advertisement to which you refer."

"So, you deny it?"

"I neither confirm nor deny it, sir. I was not aware I was being compelled to refute or admit to an action."

Cramer's face had reddened, which often happens when he visits the brownstone. "The department has no reports of gunshots having been fired last night in the vicinity referred to right here," Cramer said, still brandishing the newspaper.

"Then perhaps the advertisement was written by someone who was ill-advised," Wolfe said.

"You don't own up to being the ad's author?"

Wolfe sighed. "All right. Let us for the present stipulate that I did indeed create the advertisement. What would you assume from that action?"

"That there is funny business going on in that neighborhood. First there was the Horstmann episode, second, a man was found dead of a gunshot wound and was wedged under a North River pier, and third there are claims of shots having been fired in the same general area, all within days of one another."

"Have your men been canvassing the neighborhood?"

"Only in a cursory way," Cramer admitted, having calmed down. "So far there have been no leads whatever in the death of the man found under that pier, an individual without a police record and who appeared to have no enemies. The same could be said of Horstmann—a man with no record and without apparent enemies. Look, why don't you tell me what you know? I feel as if I'm groping in the dark and have no flashlight."

Wolfe paused to drink beer and asked if Cramer wanted something. The inspector shook his head. From years of working with my boss, I knew he was at a dead end, and I could tell that he was about to open up to the inspector.

"All right, sir, we both are groping in the dark, to use your phrase. First, it appears Theodore was suspicious of some of the individuals in a bar on Tenth Avenue across the street where he had taken up residence recently. He never shared those suspicions with me, but those with whom he had played cards in the bar's back room said Theodore felt they were plotting something. If he had specifics, he kept them to himself."

"That sounds awfully vague," Cramer remarked.

"I would normally agree, except that the man whose body was found under the pier also was part of Theodore's bridge group, and he shared Theodore's suspicions about the activities of some of those in the bar, at least a number of whom are longshoremen."

I could tell by Cramer's expression that this piece of news jolted him. "Most of the longshoremen are solid citizens," Cramer said, recovering. "But as with any other group, they have had some bad apples over the years, too."

"Has the department run into problems along the docks?" Wolfe asked.

"Not particularly. Oh, there have been the usual fights that are common on the piers, really minor stuff, but Homicide didn't get involved because there were no murders."

"And now there is one."

"Yes. We've been investigating the death of the victim, Chester Miller, who I didn't realize was a friend of Horstmann's until just now," Cramer said. "So far, we have gotten no leads in the Miller murder."

"I believe this situation goes deeper than you are aware," Wolfe told the inspector. "You should hear from Archie." As he said that, Wolfe ran a finger along one side of his nose, a signal that it was time for me to appear.

"I thought you told me Goodwin was out."

"He was, but . . . oh, come in Archie," Wolfe said as I entered the office.

"My God you look like hell!" Cramer said.

"I don't feel any so great, either, but I appreciate your concern, Inspector." Marshaling as much dignity as I could, I went over and sat at my desk, trying to ignore Cramer gawking at my puss and the top of my head.

"Mr. Goodwin has become yet another victim of the violence in that district known as Hell's Kitchen," Wolfe said. "Archie, describe to the inspector the events that caused your injuries."

It appeared that Wolfe really wanted to show all of our cards to Cramer. That being the case, I unloaded everything, including the behavior of longshoremen in McCready's, the questionable goings-on at the National Export Lines pier, my being tailed and mugged, and my firing the shot that apparently hit one of my attackers.

"And you can't identify those men?" Cramer asked.

"No, I cannot. I never got a clear look at either of them, although I did see one up close in a shadowy profile—the guy who clubbed me. They each were of medium build, and neither one did much more than mutter. For all I know, they could have been foreign."

Cramer turned his attention to Wolfe. "I want to know what kind of reaction you get from this ad in the *Gazette*," he demanded, jabbing an index finger at the wrinkled newspaper rolled up in his fist.

"Inspector, you often have accused me of obfuscating. Today, I, along with Mr. Goodwin, have been transparent and have withheld nothing from you. However, there are limits to my cooperation. Assuming we get responses to the advertisement, I will consider them and decide upon a course of action."

"Balls! It's the department that should be deciding a course of action, not you!" Cramer fumed. "Look where it has gotten you so far. Your orchid guy in a coma, one man shot dead, and Goodwin here looking like he was used for a punching bag. I can tell you one thing: We'll be canvassing the hospitals to see if anyone got admitted in the last day with a bullet wound to a lower leg or ankle. And we may or may not share information with you on anything we learn."

Wolfe considered the inspector, who had stood and was eyeing the wastebasket as a possible target for his cigar. Showing great restraint, he returned the stogie to his breast pocket and stormed out without a word.

"I would call that conversation a mixed bag," I told Wolfe after I returned from closing the front door behind Cramer. "I'm surprised you opened up to him, and I am not surprised at his reaction when you drew the line."

"Call our conversation what you will, Archie. As to your surprise at my openness, let us concede that we are stymied," Wolfe said. "The inspector has resources far greater than our own, and you know as well as I do that it would be folly for us not to utilize them."

"Point taken. By the way, I don't think I am in any kind of shape to trot down to the *Gazette*'s offices and pick up any responses that our ad might have gotten."

"I already have attended to that," Wolfe said. "When you were asleep, I telephoned Saul, and he will go to the newspaper office tonight and collect whatever information we have received from the publication's readers."

That is just like Wolfe. He often doesn't bother to fill me in on what he's doing. I started to react but gave it up; I knew any comment from me would fall upon deaf ears.

CHAPTER 19

Saul Panzer, who knew the rigid schedule on which the brownstone operates, waited until just before nine o'clock to telephone, which meant that Wolfe and I were in the office with our post-prandial coffee.

"The *Gazette* ad drew a half-dozen responses," he told me. "Should I bring them over?" I relayed the question to Wolfe, who nodded. Twenty minutes later, the doorbell rang, and I admitted Saul, clad as usual in a well-worn gray suit and a more-or-less matching flat cap.

He looked me over and shook his head. "It looks like you've got quite a story to tell," he said. "Do I want to hear it?"

"You will eventually, but not right now," I told him as we went into the office and Saul planted himself in the red leather chair.

Wolfe, who is always glad to see Saul, asked, "Can Archie get you something to drink?"

"A scotch on the rocks would suit me fine," our colleague said, grinning at me. I fulfilled my role as bartender and Saul took a sip and nodded his approval. He reached into his jacket pocket and pulled out several sheets of paper.

"Not exactly what I would call a bumper crop," he said to Wolfe. "Want to read them?"

"Why don't you do the reading?" was the response. "Archie and I are good listeners."

Saul unfolded one of the sheets. "This guy writes, 'I was walking with my girlfriend down along the riverfront when we heard what sounded like a gunshot coming from a block or so to the east on Fifth-Sixth Street. And then we saw a man running east. We did not want to get close to him, so we hurried away to the south.'

"That's all there is," Saul said.

"Fifty-Sixth Street was of course mentioned in the ad," I said.

"There was nothing substantive in that report," Wolfe stated. "What is next?"

"Three of the others are similar," Saul went on, "although I can read them if you like."

Wolfe shook his head, and Saul continued. "The gist of each is that the writer—only men responded to the ad—said he heard what he thought was a gunshot, and none of them added any helpful details.

"Here's one, though, that might be of interest:

"'I had just come out of a bar on Fifty-Sixth, half a block west of Eleventh Avenue, but I was sober, having had only one drink. I started to walk toward Eleventh when two men on the other side of the street seemed to be staggering and groaning. At first, I figured they both were drunk, but then I realized one of them apparently had been hurt and was limping. He yelled something that sounded like "aaugh! *mein bein, mein bein*," while the other man was propping him up and trying to help him walk.

"'I crossed over and asked if I could help them, but they wouldn't even speak to me. They just growled and kept on walking, or I should say staggering, while the one who was hurt kept groaning and dragging one leg as he was pulled along. A couple of other pedestrians heard them and stared, but that was all. The two got to Tenth and turned north. I followed them at a distance, and they kept going north, eventually going into an apartment building. Maybe I should have done something, but I couldn't figure out what to do, so I went home to my flat, and later I saw the item in the *Gazette*. I am not sure what I witnessed is part of the same event that was referred to.'"

"I suppose that the writer signed his name?" I asked.

"He did, along with an address and phone number," Saul said, holding up the sheet. "He is one Jason Knowles," Saul said, holding up the sheet that also gave his phone number and an address on Eighth Avenue."

"Call Mr. Knowles," Wolfe ordered me. "I would like to meet the gentleman, tomorrow at eleven a.m., if possible."

Being ever helpful, I dialed the number, and a deep male voice answered, "Knowles."

"You are the one who responded to an advertisement in the *Gazette*?"

"Yes, that's me," he answered in an eager voice.

"The ad was placed by a private investigator, Nero Wolfe, and he—"

"Oh yes, I have certainly read about him, in several articles over the years," Knowles said, sounding impressed.

"He would like to see you and hear your story. Would tomorrow morning at eleven be convenient?"

Knowles paused before responding. "Uh, well . . . I have a sales job on the floor at Macy's Herald Square in the men's department, but . . . yes, I could take an early lunch. They give me some flexibility. Where should we meet?"

I explained that Nero Wolfe rarely leaves home and gave the address of the brownstone, which I pointed out was not far from Herald Square.

"All right, yes, I can be there," Knowles said. "Can I assume there is a reward, as was mentioned in the ad?"

"That will be determined by Nero Wolfe," I said.

"And you are. . . ?"

"Archie Goodwin, an associate of Mr. Wolfe's."

"Oh yes, of course. I believe I have seen your name in the newspapers, too."

I let that comment pass, maybe out of modesty, although I've never thought of myself as being particularly modest. I told Knowles that we would expect him tomorrow.

The next morning the bell rang at 11 a.m. sharp, a point in our alleged witness's favor. I swung open the front door to reveal a well dressed man of about forty whose short stature belied his deep voice. When I say well-dressed, I mean he looks like what you would expect from someone who sold menswear at Macy's: He sported a three-piece, charcoal pin-striped suit along with a silk red-and-gray striped tie and red handkerchief sprouting from his breast pocket.

"Please come in, Mr. Knowles," I said. "I'm Archie Goodwin." If he was startled by my appearance, he didn't show it, thanking me and stepping inside.

I walked our visitor down the hall to the office, directing him to the red leather chair. "Mr. Wolfe should be in shortly," I told him.

"Shortly" turned out to be less than a half-minute. Wolfe strode in, placed a raceme of orchids in the vase on his desk, sat, and considered our guest. "Mr. Knowles, would you like something to drink? I am having beer."

"Nothing for me, thanks, I have to be at work later," Knowles said. As had been the case when he saw me, the man did not seem in the least surprised by Wolfe's appearance.

"We found your report to be interesting," Wolfe said as Fritz brought in two bottles of chilled beer and a stein. "Are you often out on the streets of Hell's Kitchen in the evening?"

"I live alone, I'm a bachelor, since my divorce, Mr. Wolfe. And I have gotten into the habit of going out after dinner for a drink in any one of a number of bars within walking distance of my co-op on Eighth Avenue. I'm by no means a heavy drinker—I usually find that one rye is enough, or on occasions, two. They help me get to sleep. And I also like the exercise."

"When you encountered those two men, do I assume you were taking a post-drink walk before returning home?"

"That is correct," Knowles said. "I love the street life in the city, and I usually take a different route each night."

"You do not fear danger on the streets after dark?"

"By no means. I have been walking around that area at night for several years, and nothing out-of-the-ordinary has ever happened."

"Back to those two men you encountered," Wolfe said after taking a drink of beer. "Had you seen them before?"

"Never," Knowles said.

"How would you describe them?"

"I really didn't get a good look at either one. I guess they were of about medium build. As far as their ages, I couldn't hazard a guess in the dark."

"Do you speak German?"

"I don't," Knowles replied, wearing a puzzled expression. "I do know enough French to get by in Paris, which I like to visit, but that is my only foreign language."

"I believe that in your response to my advertisement, you wrote that one of the men used the words *mein bein*."

"As least that's what they sounded like to me," Knowles said. "I may not have been pronouncing the words right."

"Your pronunciation was correct. Those words, spoken in German, mean 'my leg.'"

"I am not surprised to hear that, because the one who cried out was limping, as though something had happened to his leg. Was that because of the gunshot referred to in your ad?"

"That is very possible," Wolfe said. "Before you saw those men, did you hear a gunshot?"

"Honesty compels me to say no," Knowles said, "even though I realize that may jeopardize my chance of getting any reward."

"You mentioned that on occasion you have stopped in several bars in the Hell's Kitchen area. Is one of those establishments McCready's on Tenth Avenue?"

"It is. I was there once, oh, probably close to a year ago now."

"What was your impression of the establishment?"

"Frankly, I did not like it," Knowles said. "Overall, the crowd in there seemed to be pretty rough and loud. Not nearly as friendly as other places I've frequented. From some of the conversation I overheard, I gathered that a lot of the patrons are longshoremen. I suppose that's not surprising, given the tavern's proximity to all those piers that line the Hudson."

"Did anything else strike you about McCready's?" Wolfe asked.

"I . . . don't think so. Oh, come to think of it, I do remember hearing some foreign language spoken in there."

"There are many displaced persons in New York now," Wolfe said. "Have you noticed any of them in your neighborhood?"

Knowles wrinkled a brow. "Well, yes, I suppose I actually might have, perhaps without realizing it. On the streets and in some of the shops and restaurants, I've heard other languages being spoken with increased frequency, languages I of course don't know and would not try to guess at, except maybe German. And judging by the appearance of the speakers, they are dressed in a way that indicates their lives probably have not have been easy ones. We've all read about the terrible problems of the displaced persons and how they have struggled to get to the United States."

"Two more questions, Mr. Knowles: You mentioned following those two men as they went north on Tenth Avenue and entered an apartment building. Where was that building and what did it look like?"

"It was . . . let's see . . . just north of Fifty-Eighth Street, and it wasn't a very tall building, maybe five or six stories. Not what I would call luxurious by any means. And now that I think of it, the place was just across the street from that bar you had asked me about, McCready's."

"Indeed. Archie, please give Mr. Knowles one hundred dollars from petty cash and make a note of it. Thank you for coming, sir," Wolfe said, rising and walking out, almost surely headed for the kitchen.

His host's abrupt departure seemed surprising to Jason Knowles, but any unease he might have felt was more than offset by the money I handed to him.

"I was afraid that what I told Mr. Wolfe might not have seemed useful to him," he said.

"I do not always understand my boss's thinking, but then, he is a genius and I most definitely am not. If nothing else, you may have confirmed some of his suspicions or surmises."

"Well, what happened that night was a most unsettling experience for me," Knowles said. "I wish I could somehow have been of help."

"You may have been of more help than you think," I told him as I saw him to the front door of the brownstone.

CHAPTER 20

After Jason Knowles left, I went to the kitchen and found Wolfe conferring with Fritz about lunch. "Our visitor has departed and you are free to go back to the office," I told him. He never likes to dismiss people, preferring to exit the office, leaving the good-byes to me.

"Well, what did you think of Mr. Knowles's report?" I posed when we were resettled in the office.

"I found him to be trustworthy and moderately helpful."

"Helpful in what way?"

"First, he in essence confirmed that at least one of the two men he encountered on the street that night is a speaker of German. Second, he saw the two men enter the Elmont, which would suggest one or both of them reside in that building."

"Which would seem to indicate that the place is a hot-bed of something or other," I said, which was hardly being helpful.

"Get Mr. Cramer," Wolfe ordered. I dialed a number I had memorized years ago as Wolfe picked up his instrument and I stayed on the line.

"Cramer!" came the bark I had come to expect from the homicide inspector.

"This is Nero Wolfe. I have come into the possession of information you may find of interest."

"Before I ask what that information is, what is its source?"

"No, sir. My source is not germane to this discussion. Are you interested, or not?"

A drawn-out sigh moved across the wire, followed by a silence that lasted several seconds. "All right, shoot, Wolfe. And you had better not be wasting my time."

"Have I ever wasted your time, sir? Before I move ahead, a question: Has any hospital in Manhattan reported the admission of an individual with a gunshot wound to the leg or ankle in the last few days?"

"They have not—and yes, we've been checking."

"I suggest the person you seek is in the Elmont apartment building on Tenth Avenue near Fifty-Eighth Street."

"Is this individual of yours a resident of the Elmont?" Cramer asked.

"That is probable but not definite."

"And I suppose you got this information from one of the people who answered your ad in the *Gazette*?"

"It is immaterial where and how I received the information, sir. But I felt it my duty to share it with you."

"Your duty, hah! When have you seen it a duty to do anything to help the department?"

"I believe I am helping the department with what I have told you."

"I will be the judge of that," Cramer said.

"As you wish," Wolfe replied, but he was speaking to no one, as the inspector had hung up.

"It seems our top homicide cop is looking a gift horse in the mouth," I said.

Wolfe made a face, as he often does in reaction to comments I come out with. "If you insist upon resorting to clichés, I will reply in kind and suggest that Mr. Cramer would be wise to saddle and ride that horse of which you speak. Are you prepared to give odds on whether he orders a search of the Elmont apartments?"

"Sure, I'll make it three-to-one that homicide cops will be going door-to-door in that tired old building looking for someone with a Marley .38 bullet in his leg. And the reason I say homicide cops will do the sweep is that all this is surely tied to Chester Miller's murder."

"For once, I cannot argue either with those odds or with your reasoning."

"Thanks a lot for the vote of confidence. As you have said in the past, even a stopped clock is correct twice a day."

Wolfe let that remark pass. "I suggest that you telephone Mr. Cohen." Whenever Wolfe "suggests" something to me, that is tantamount to an order. "Let me guess what you want me to tell him," I said. "That the police are conducting a sweep of a certain apartment building on Tenth Avenue near Fifty-Eighth Street, hoping to locate a man with a gunshot wound who may be connected to a murder."

"Mr. Cohen will of course want to know how we come to have this information."

"And when Lon asks, as he will, I will reply that we are not at liberty to divulge our sources."

"Satisfactory," Wolfe said, opening an orchid catalog that had arrived with the morning mail.

Lon picked up the phone on the first ring. "Cohen!" he snapped.

"And a pleasant good day to you, too."

"Now what favor are you looking for this time?"

"That is hardly a way to greet a guy who is coming to you with information."

"Pardon my skepticism, but I always get leery when you tell me that you have information for me. It usually means I have to cough something up for you."

"I am cut to the quick. Here I am with something you might find interesting."

"Okay, I'm listening," Lon said. "What's the information that you seem to be so proud of?"

I then proceeded to, in essence, give him the same phrasing I read to Wolfe.

"And just where did you learn this tidbit?" was the response.

"We are not at liberty to reveal our resources."

"How often have we at the *Gazette*—and every other paper in the country, as well—heard those words? And now I have to listen to them from an old friend and poker-playing buddy, no less."

"Well, you are hearing them again from this old friend and poker-playing buddy. I thought you would be delighted to get this information, and delivered to you on a platter, no less."

"Some platter! You're not going to tell me this came from Inspector Cramer, are you?"

"I am not. And I am also not asking you for something in return for what I consider to be a good news tip."

"We will be the judge of that. Because of past conversations you and I have had, I assume the building to which you refer on Tenth Avenue is none other than the Elmont."

"As I've often said, you are a fast study."

That brought a snort on the other end of the line. "Cramer will be madder than a wet hen if one or two of our reporters show up while his men are scouring the Elmont."

"So what? Surely, you are not about to tell me that the mighty *Gazette* is going to be intimidated by the growls and scowls of one Lionel T. Cramer of Homicide."

"At the moment, I am not going to tell you anything," Lon said. "I believe you have a subscription to our fine product. I will let its pages speak for themselves."

"Spoken like a staunch representative of the Fourth Estate," I told him. The response I got was a word his newspaper would never print, followed by a click that told me the conversation had been terminated.

CHAPTER 21

It would have been unrealistic of me to expect that evening's *Gazette* to carry anything related to the Elmont or the man with a bullet in his leg. But the next morning, just before Wolfe came down from the plant rooms at eleven, I was out on the stoop when the carrier on his battered bicycle delivered our copy of the paper's early edition.

"Nice to see you, Mr. Goodwin," he said.

"Good to see you, too, Eddie. Right on time as usual."

"Hey, I've gotta be on time. My real job is driving a scrap metal truck over in Brooklyn, and it begins at twelve thirty." He cycled off along Thirty-Fifth Street, slinging papers with the accuracy of a relief pitcher onto the stoops of the shoulder-to-shoulder brownstones that line the block.

I opened our copy of the *Gazette* on the steps and found what I was looking for at the bottom of page seven, under the headline **Homicide Cops Find Wounded Man in Hotel Who**

May Be Murder Suspect. The article identified the guy I had shot as William Hartz, fifty-eight, calling him "a displaced person from the Sudetenland region of Czechoslovakia who apparently entered the United States on a falsified visa."

The piece went on to say that Hartz had not reported his injury and that he had a .38 revolver in his apartment, the same caliber weapon that was used to kill Chester Miller, according to the autopsy. The last sentence read, "The police refused to divulge how they learned of Hartz and his location."

I went inside and laid the paper on Wolfe's desk blotter. I knew Inspector Cramer was kept apprised of any newspaper coverage involving the Homicide Squad, so it figured to be a matter of minutes before we received a call from him.

Wolfe came down from his morning visit with the orchids and scanned the *Gazette* article as he rang for beer. "You realize who is about to (a) telephone us or (b) ring the doorbell," I told him, receiving a glare for my trouble. Just as Fritz brought in the beer, option (b) came to pass.

"Good morning," I said to Cramer, swinging open the door to admit him. I received a glare in return and he stormed by, heading down the hall to the office with me in close pursuit.

As I got to the door, I watched the inspector zero in on the red leather chair and land with a thump.

"Good morning sir," Wolfe said calmly.

"And exactly what is good about it?" Cramer fired back. "Sometimes I feel like my department is being run by remote control from this goddamned office."

"Judging by this article," Wolfe said, picking up the *Gazette,* "it would appear that your minions have made some progress in the investigation of Mr. Miller's death."

"Maybe, but we seem to be operating in a goldfish bowl, thanks to you and your friend Cohen. My men had just got to that Tenth Avenue flop house and began their sweep when three—count 'em three—*Gazette* reporters show up, along with a photographer."

"The article contained no pictures," Wolfe said.

"You are damned right, it didn't. At least we shagged the photog off, but the reporters were harder to discourage, like barnacles on the hull of a ship."

"Do you feel you have your killer, sir?"

"Hell, I wouldn't swear to it, but he's being grilled right now. Goodwin, I want you to come downtown and look at this character through the one-way glass and make a definite identification."

"I don't know why you need me. As Mr. Wolfe told you, I'm the one who shot him in the leg or ankle, so it's got to be the same guy."

"Calf, just above the ankle. But we need to make it official so we can at least charge him with assault before we work toward a murder rap."

I looked at Wolfe, who blinked twice, giving the okay for me to go to headquarters. "I look like hell," I told Cramer.

He resisted a smile. "Who's going to care?" he said.

"Thanks for the sympathy. When do you want me down there?"

"How about this afternoon, say three o'clock."

"Okay, but remember it was dark when I got mugged, so I didn't get a really good look at either guy. I just saw one in a silhouetted profile."

"We'll take our chances. Do you want a cruiser to pick you up?"

"No, I'll grab a cab. Nothing personal, Inspector, but riding in squad cars always gives me a complex."

"Suit yourself. And before I go, Wolfe, I'm not happy with the way you sicced those reporters on my men."

"I have always felt you and your officers are capable of dealing with newspaper people. Besides, I know you value a free and unfettered press."

Cramer glowered at Wolfe but rose and walked out without uttering a word. I followed him to the door and let the silence continue.

"He usually yells and throws a cigar at the wastebasket when he leaves. I do hope he isn't ill," I said to Wolfe.

"The inspector has a lot on his mind, and I believe what has been transpiring in Hell's Kitchen troubles him greatly, as it does me."

I started to ask Wolfe what he meant but was interrupted by the ringing of the telephone. It was Lily Rowan.

"I've been back from visiting my cousin in St. Louis for three days now, and have not heard a single word out of you, my dear Escamillo. I was concerned that you had grown tired of my company or had found someone else in my absence."

I mentioned Lily earlier, and I should add to that she is beautiful, rich through inheritance, and, by her own definition, lazy, although I don't agree with the lazy part. She gives scads of money and lots of time to needy causes. She and I go out often—to plays, the opera, hockey games, dinner, and dancing. And just so you don't get any ideas, I always pay.

"Me, grow tired of your company? Surely you jest. And no, I definitely haven't found someone else. I have no reason to go looking."

"Then why haven't I heard from you?"

"Well . . . something has come up that—"

"Archie Goodwin—level with me!"

When Lily calls me by my full name, I know she demands an answer. "Okay, I ran into some trouble the other night, and I'm, well, a little bit banged up."

"*A little banged up!* I am coming over right now!"

"No, we're about to have lunch, and—"

"Put Nero Wolfe on the line, this instant."

"Lily wishes to speak to you," I said. Wolfe normally is not comfortable around women, but he has always made an exception for Lily, probably because the first time they met, which was years ago, she asked to see all those orchids up on the roof. To this day, he sends her orchids on her birthday.

"Yes, Miss Rowan," he said into the mouthpiece. "By all means you are welcome. We are having sweetbreads in bécha-mel sauce with truffle and chervil, beet and watercress salad, and strawberries Romanoff. Yes, one fifteen." Wolfe nodded to me to pick up as he cradled his receiver.

"So, you up and invited yourself to lunch?"

"Desperate times call for desperate measures, my dear," she said.

"Well, be prepared to see a wreck of a man," I complained.

"I am sure that I will be able to stand it. Besides, no matter how bad you look, Fritz's cuisine will more than make up for whatever shock I incur."

"Just don't say later that you had not been warned."

At one o'clock, the front bell chimed; Lily was prompt, as usual. I could have sent Fritz to answer the door, but I thought it was best that she got a good look at me at the start of her visit, so she would have adjusted to my appearance before sitting down to eat.

"Oh, Escamillo, I was expecting to find you swathed in ban-dages from head to foot, like a walking mummy. As it is, you are . . . well, more or less bearable to the eye," she said as she stepped in and gave me a hug and a kiss.

"Aw, shucks, little lady, you say the nicest things to a feller,"

I told her. "And in return, I have to say you look terrific, as you always do."

I knew she was dying to ask me how I came to look this way, but that would have to come later. She knew from past dining experiences in the brownstone that Wolfe never allows business to infringe upon the conversation at the table. And as usual today, he set the topic for the meal, which was the westward movement in the United States. "This trend has been discussed for decades, ever since the newspaper editor Horace Greeley is supposed to have written, 'Go West, young man,' in the 1860s," Wolfe said. "Transportation challenges stifled the move west until this century, and it now appears to be occurring with alacrity. California was our fifth-most-populous state in 1940, and it surely will surpass Archie's very own Ohio when last year's final census numbers get released."

"I have been to California twice, Mr. Wolfe," Lily said, "and I can see its attraction. It would not surprise me if someday more people live there than in any other state."

"I agree," Wolfe responded, and we were off on a discussion of the effects of weather and the local culture on population swings. I did not have a lot to add, other than to mention that I had been to California once and did not have a burning desire to return.

After we had finished our strawberries Romanoff, Wolfe rose, saying "Pardon me, but I must excuse myself to consult with Fritz on a number of culinary matters." That was his way of saying that he knew Lily wanted to learn more about what had happened to me, so the two of us went into the office with cups of coffee.

"Don't go to your desk," she said, "but come and sit with me over here." She patted the cushions of the sofa against one wall. I followed orders and we parked side by side.

"All right, Escamillo, tell me exactly how you have come to look as you do. I want to know everything, and I do mean *everything*."

I unloaded the works, starting with Theodore's suspicions and his subsequent mugging and continuing through the bridge games at McCready's, my stay at the Elmont, questionable activities on the docks, the shooting of Chester Miller, my own mugging and concussion, and my gunshot that crippled the man being identified as William Hartz.

Lily remained silent throughout my recitation. When I finished, she shook her head in wonder. "What about Theodore Horstmann?"

"He's still in a coma, and Doc Vollmer is closely monitoring his condition. My boss has a substitute gardener working with him on the orchids."

"Does the doctor have a prognosis?"

"He is taking what I would call a wait-and-see attitude. He claims there's been a slight improvement in Theodore's condition, and he also says he has known of cases in which a person in a coma can fully recover even after a long period of being unconscious."

"How about you, Escamillo? What does the doctor say regarding your concussion?"

"I'm supposed to take it easy for at least a week, meaning no physical exertion, and I can eat normally and drink plenty of liquids."

"Do you think you will be able to 'take it easy' for a whole week?" Lily asked, arching an eyebrow.

"Well, it might help if you came over every day and provided me with some personal care."

"Is that so? I suppose you also want me to wear a nurse's uniform."

"Well . . . since you mentioned it, I think that would look very, very—"

"Never mind! It is clear to me you have a concussion that causes you to live in a fantasy world."

"I really expected more sympathy from you. After all, look at all that I have been through."

"Poor baby," she said, placing a slender, manicured hand on my forehead. "You don't seem to be at all feverish."

"Must be that it comes and goes."

"Maybe, and speaking of going, I have to be off, my dear. I have a meeting of the board at the women's shelter in Brooklyn."

"I will try my best to survive in your absence," I told her.

"I have no doubt that you will, my darling Escamillo," she replied, planting a kiss on my forehead and striding out, high heels clicking on the hall floor.

After Lily had gone, I put in a call to the folks at Yellow Cab, asking for my favorite driver, Herb Aronson, and giving my name. I was told by an efficient female voice with a New Jersey accent that "We will attempt to reach Mr. Aronson, Mr. Goodwin." Within ten minutes, the telephone jangled. "Hi, Archie, long time, no hear from you."

"Yes, it's been a while. Where are you, Herb?"

"Call box on Eighteenth Street. If you need me to ferry you someplace, I can be at your place before your watch makes fifteen rotations."

"Fine. I'll be waiting out in front."

Herb was good for his word. Fourteen minutes later by my watch, he pulled up at the curb and stuck his head out the window. "Looks like you've had some trouble lately," he observed.

"I'll tell you about it as we go to police headquarters," I said.

Herb Aronson is chatty but not nosy, and he silently listened to my edited tale of woe as we drove south to 240 Centre Street, where the nerve center of the New York City police department stood majestically, looking like a state capitol, complete with an elaborate dome.

"That's quite a story, Archie," Herb said as I climbed out of his taxi. "I'll be right here when they get through with you. Good luck."

I knew the way to Inspector Cramer's office, having been there too many times for my taste. I waited in his anteroom, my only company being his grim-faced secretary, who was clattering away on her ancient Smith-Corona.

After ten minutes, the door to the inner sanctum swung open and the man himself came out, coatless and with sleeves rolled up. "All right, Goodwin, follow me," he said. "We'll take a look at our man through the one-way glass."

We went into an unadorned room that had one wall of glass, which looked on another plain room with a steel table and two chairs. "That's Hartz," Cramer said, indicating a man in prison garb seated on one side of the table, facing another man who turned out to be a plainclothes cop I didn't recognize.

Cramer pushed a button. This alerted the cop in the next room, who told his charge to "Stand up, walk once around the table, stop, face left, face right, face that way." I was able to view Hartz head on and in two profiles. It was the first guy who had been tailing me, all right. I had gotten that quick look at him in profile just before his trailing partner gave me the concussion. I told Cramer.

"A tough nut," the inspector said. "We can't get one damned word out of him, even with threats of him being charged with murder."

"You figure he's the one who plugged Chester Miller?"

"Yeah, but we can't prove it. We got his .38 when we searched his room, all right, but we've got no shell to compare it to, although the autopsy said the wound was almost surely caused by a .38. And as you probably read, the bullet that killed Miller exited his head and is God-knows-where now. We don't even know where the poor sap was shot before his body was dumped in the Hudson."

"So now what?"

"Based on you identifying him, we can hold him on a battery charge, as well as his being in this country without a legal visa."

"Has he got a lawyer?"

"Oddly, no. He knows he's entitled to one, a public defender at the very least; he understands English, although he doesn't speak it very well. But he seems content to sit in his cell with his lips sealed. And nobody has come forward to help him. The guy has been hung out to dry by his friends, if you want to call them friends."

"You need me for anything else?"

"No, go home and rest. You still don't look all that great."

"Thanks for your candor," I told him, glad to be leaving the building.

CHAPTER 22

The next several days dragged by. I am not used to sitting around doing nothing more than opening the mail and typing a few letters for Wolfe. I once told him that I am supposed to be a man of action to complement his man of brains, but now the most action I'm getting is standing and walking over to the three-drawer cabinet to enter the orchid germination records that Theodore's temporary replacement, Carl Willis, brings down every afternoon. I had once told Wolfe "that if you keep a keg of dynamite around the house, you've got to expect some noise sooner or later. That's what I am, a keg of dynamite."

On the subject of Willis, I had no idea how he was getting along upstairs with the orchids, because he is as closed-mouthed as Horstmann. And when I have asked Wolfe how the new man is working out, he just grunts. Unfortunately, I have never learned to accurately translate his various grunts.

Speaking of Wolfe, he just entered the office after his morning session with the orchids and rang for beer. After going through the morning mail, which I had opened and stacked on his desk, he cleared his throat, which sometimes happens when he was prepared to speak.

"Archie, on some occasions in the past, you have accused me not keeping you apprised of my plans when we are working on a case."

"On 'some occasions', you say? Make that 'lots of occasions'!"

"As you wish," he sighed. "I am about to bring you up-to-date."

"Please do. I feel like my joints are getting rusty from lack of stimulation."

"Because of your enforced inactivity, I have asked Saul to continue our investigation into the series of events triggered by the attack upon Theodore. He will be coming over sometime today to confer with you."

"Swell. He can feel free to pick my brain. Nobody else is doing anything with it."

Wolfe ignored that shot and picked up his latest book, *Roosevelt and Hopkins*, by Robert Sherwood. I returned to typing up his dictation from the day before, making sure to hit the keys extra hard, which always irritates him. For years he has offered to buy a noiseless typewriter, but—perhaps out of sheer perversity—I have insisted that I'm comfortable with the machine we have.

After lunch and after Wolfe had gone up to the plant rooms, Saul Panzer arrived and we settled down in the office, me at my desk and Saul in one of the yellow chairs. "Well, you look marginally better," he observed.

"I'll take marginally. I understand from Wolfe that you are going to be filling in for me on the street."

"Hey, I'm not trying to horn in on your—"

"It's okay," I said, waving his comment aside. "I know damned well that for at least the next several days, I am not going to be out on the streets fighting the forces of evil. I am turning that task over to you."

"Remind me to thank you for your confidence. Of course, I know some of what's been going on, but for now, assume I'm coming into all of this fresh," Saul said. "Don't be afraid to tell me about any details—or people—you think I might already have knowledge of."

"I probably don't have to tell you this, but I will anyway: Keep a piece with you at all times. These people, whoever they may be, are not playing games."

"Give me your thoughts about the characters you've run into."

"I'll start with Liam McCready, who runs the pub bearing that name."

"I've seen him, but that's all. We've never spoken."

"He's what I think of as the typical Irishman, and that's how I think he sees himself, too: Hail-fellow-well-met, full of the blarney, convivial, colorful. Good qualities for a barkeep. Makes you feel welcome, whether or not he's being sincere. Would I trust him? My vote is still out on that.

"Next is the super at the Elmont, a dismal and seedy-looking guy named Erwin Bauer, whose personality is the polar opposite of McCready's. He's not very forthcoming, to say the least. Maybe I'm being overly suspicious, but he seems like a man who is hiding something.

"Then there's that Italian grocer across Tenth Avenue from the Elmont, who told Orrie, as you recall, that the building is a 'very bad place, *cattivo*.' You will also recall that when Orrie pressed the grocer, the guy clammed up. Maybe you can pry something more out of him. You have the finesse that Orrie lacks."

"Maybe," Saul said. "I wondered at the time why Orrie didn't lean harder on the Italian."

"I would also suggest you stop by and see my old friend Charlie King at the Cabot and Sons pier on the North River. See if he's learned any more about the goings-on at the docks of his neighbor, the National Export Lines. It seems they could well be smuggling DPs."

"I'll check in with King, who I've met a few times over the years. Good guy. Think I should drop in at McCready's? I'm not sure the owner will remember me from the couple of times I played bridge there. I could sit at the bar, have a drink or two, and see what I can sniff out."

"I suppose it's worth a try. I've got to wonder whether there's a connection among National Export, McCready's, and the Elmont involving DPs."

"What does Wolfe think?" Saul asked.

"So far, he's not sharing his thoughts on that connection with me, which is hardly unusual for him. He seems to like keeping me in the dark."

"Right now, he's probably worried about your physical condition," Saul offered.

"I suppose that's possible. Anything else that I can tell you?"

"Not that comes to mind, but as I nose around, I'm sure questions will arise. I suppose you won't be joining us for poker on Thursday."

"As much as it pains me to say, I'm going to sit this one out. I have a hard enough time trying to take money from you and Lon Cohen when I'm healthy. In the state I find myself at the moment, it would be child's play for you two hustlers. And Durkin and Bill Gore and Bascom probably would pick my pocket as well."

"Hustlers, indeed!" Saul snapped. "We all just play the cards that we are dealt."

"I won't argue the point. But by next week, I plan to be back, ready to take on all comers."

"I'll warn the others of your impending return. In the meantime, get plenty of rest and think good thoughts," Saul said, rising to leave. "I will check in with you and your boss when I have something newsworthy to report."

When Wolfe descended from his playtime with the orchids, I gave him a report on my visit to police headquarters and my meeting with Saul. "You have no doubt that this man Hartz was the one who was following you?"

"None whatever. As you know, I'm good with faces, and I had a brief but good look at him in profile, before I got clobbered by the guy who was behind him. Cramer says they've grilled Hartz for hours, but from what he told me, it seems like the thug has buttoned his yap tighter than a mafioso on the witness stand."

Wolfe has never liked my analogies, if that's what I just came out with. He has always felt that I play fast and loose with the English language, so I like to spit things out just to see the expressions on his face, and I got a dandy reaction this time. Hey, when a guy who likes action is stuck on the bench while the game is going on, he's got to find ways to amuse himself.

"Saul says he'll check in from time to time with developments, if and when there are any," I told Wolfe. "If I may ask, what kind of instructions have you given him?"

Wolfe closed his eyes and paused several seconds before responding, so I knew that what was coming would be a lulu: "I told Saul," he purred, pausing for effect, "that he was to act in the light of experience as guided by intelligence."

He was of course tweaking yours truly with a phrase he had so often used on me when I questioned how I was to proceed on a case. I tried to think of a response, but none came to mind, so I did as I have in the past when holding lousy poker hands. I folded.

This frustrated keg of dynamite was on the verge of going off the next day when a call came from Saul Panzer at a little before 11 a.m. "I may have an opening of sorts," he said. "I'm home now, but this morning, I paid a visit to that Italian grocer across Tenth Avenue from the Elmont, and as closed-mouthed as he is, I think I have found a way that he can be loosened up."

"I hope you're not planning to get rough with the poor guy."

"Hey, you know me better than that, Archie; I am the gentlest of men. Turns out that our grocer—his name is Enzo Paolucci—is somewhat cash-strapped. My advice is that based on my conversation with him, he could be persuaded to open up if some greenbacks were to come his way. Mr. Wolfe may not want to do that, but I have a feeling Mr. Paolucci could, with the right stimulus, be persuaded to visit the brownstone and talk to your boss, who is a far better interviewer than I am."

"What makes you think he would have anything interesting to say?"

"As I talked to him, I could sense with the right approach—and cash—he might talk about those people that he told Orrie were *cattivo* and 'very bad.'"

"Hell, it's worth a try. We aren't getting anywhere as it is. I'll toss it to Wolfe and see what he thinks."

I waited until he descended from the plant rooms and had taken his first sip of beer before bringing Paolucci up. He leaned back and frowned.

"Is Saul where he can be reached?"

"Yes, he's at home."

"Get him."

I dialed and he answered immediately. "Mr. Wolfe would like to talk to you," I said, staying on the line.

"Good day, Saul. Archie tells me you sense Mr. Paolucci might be persuaded to share his feelings about those sometimes-secretive tenants of the Elmont who patronize his establishment."

"Yes, sir. I know that Orrie didn't get a lot out of him, and to be honest I wasn't much more successful, but I did find out that Paolucci needs money, and I suggested to him, none too subtly, that some cash might just come his way if he shared his thoughts about his customers."

"How much money do you think he is seeking?"

"I can't say for sure, but I think a C-note might be enough to loosen his tongue."

"Indeed. I suggest you pay another visit to Mr. Paolucci and determine if he would be willing to come here and allow himself to be questioned in return for a payment of one hundred dollars. I suspect you can be most persuasive when you put your mind to it without resorting to physical intimidation."

"As I told Archie, I am a gentle soul. I try to persuade with words, rather than threats. And in this case, any words I might use would be backed by the promise of the coin of the realm."

"I trust your persuasive powers," Wolfe said, cradling his instrument.

"He's off the line, but I'm still here," I told Saul. "Do you think Paolucci will want the money up front?"

"I'll go over to his place right now and find out. If I were to guess, and that's all it is—a guess—I would say he'd like to see the greenbacks first. And I have a thought: What if you give me a crisp Ben Franklin, and I then hand it to Paolucci, but only when we are in a taxi on the way over to the brownstone?"

"I like your thinking. If you were to give the jack to him

in his store, you might not be able to budge him out of the place."

"We read each other like a book, Archie. You will hear from me soon."

CHAPTER 23

That evening just before dinner, I did hear from Saul. "Barkis is willin'," he said into my receiver, to which I responded, "huh?"

"Don't tell me you've never read *David Copperfield* by Dickens," he said.

"If I ever did read any of Dickens, it must have been back in school in Ohio," I told him.

"Oh, Archie, I'm not sure there is any hope for you. Is Mr. Wolfe in the room?"

"Yep, just polishing off a beer."

"Tell you what: Repeat that phrase to him and see his reaction."

"Is this going to make me look stupid?"

"Just say it to him."

I sighed and turned to Wolfe, who was reading a book. "Saul says to tell you that 'Barkis is willin.'"

"Excellent!" Wolfe said, picking up his instrument. "When can Mr. Paolucci be here, Saul?"

"He closes up his store at nine p.m. Would nine thirty be too late?"

"Not at all. We shall expect the two of you then. Satisfactory."

I was damned if I was going to ask Wolfe the meaning of those three words, which both he and Saul were familiar with. I decided to go about finding out myself, even if it involved reading a whole damned book.

The bell rang at 9:18 p.m., and I went to the front door, swinging it open to reveal Saul Panzer and a stocky, full-faced man in his fifties with dark center-parted hair who wore a checked sport coat and a shy expression.

"Mr. Paolucci, this is Archie Goodwin, who works with Nero Wolfe, the man you are about to meet."

Paolucci held out a right hand tentatively, and I shook it. "Very nice to see you, and thanks very much for coming." He muttered a "You're welcome" as the three of us walked down the hall to the office, where Wolfe sat at his desk, closing his book.

Saul did the introductions, gesturing Paolucci to the red leather chair, which he eased into, looking at Wolfe.

"Mr. Paolucci, we appreciate you taking the time to come here tonight. Can we get you something to drink? As you see, I am having beer."

Paolucci looked at Saul, as if getting permission to speak. Saul nodded, and the grocer asked, "Would it be possible to have chianti?"

"It would," Wolfe replied, looking at me. There was no chianti on the bar cart against one wall of the office, but there were bottles of it in the extensive wine cellar in our basement. I excused myself and left. When I returned with a glass of the wine, Wolfe was saying ". . . and so you decided to come to the United States."

"Yes, sir," Paolucci said in slightly accented English. "It was 1931, and *Il Duce* had been in charge for almost ten years. I never liked his methods, and as time went by, life in Italy had become increasingly intolerable unless you were part of the *fascismo italiano*, which ran the country and made life miserable for anyone who opposed them."

"What type of work did you do?"

"Like here, I was a grocer then, in Lucca, which is in Toscana, or Tuscany, as you call it."

"I was there many years ago," Wolfe said, "but I remember it clearly. A picturesque setting."

"Yes, it was, but I came to hate Mussolini and his fascists more with each day. I finally told my wife that we had to leave Italy, and she agreed."

"That was a bold move, sir. Did you have children?"

"Not at the time. We were young, and I had inherited the store from my father, who had died in 1928. I sold it to a cousin, and with what money we got from that sale, we booked passage and came here."

"You hardly picked a good time to start anew in New York," Wolfe observed.

Paolucci nodded. "The Depression, yes, although it was every bit as bad in Europe, too. We probably would not have survived here except for family members who had come to the city from Italy years before us. They gave us a room in their flat in Brooklyn, and my brother-in-law, Ricco, got a job for me in the Fulton Fish Market downtown. It was hard work, long days. But I saved and my wife, who is a very fine seamstress, sewed clothes for women in the neighborhood. Again, long hours, hard work.

"But still, life was good here, and six years ago, when Mussolini was killed by some of his own countrymen, I celebrated by drinking a half bottle of this," Paolucci said, pointing to his glass of chianti.

"I am sure you were not alone in celebrating that event," Wolfe said. I could see exactly what my boss was doing, putting our guest at ease by getting him to reminisce before beginning any interrogation. It also probably didn't hurt Mr. Paolucci's mood that he presumably had a hundred bucks in his pocket. "Along the way, I gather you had children?" Wolfe asked.

That finally brought a smile to Paolucci's broad, Mediterranean face. "Yes, two sons, one in high school, the other two years younger."

"How were you able to get your grocery store?"

"Luck was a part of that, Mr. Wolfe. Again, my brother-in-law was a great help. He works in the wholesale vegetable and fruit business, and he knew of a man who owned a grocery store on Tenth Avenue—the one that now is my own. This man was old, he had become very ill, and he could not work any longer. He was willing to sell to me at a very good price. The purchase also included the flat above the store, where we now live."

"You have had good fortune," Wolfe said. "And your English is excellent, only slightly accented."

Another smile from the grocer. "When we came here, I was determined that I would fit in, and I worked very hard on my speaking. I had read that the better the English, the faster you will become accepted. I did not take any classes, but I have a good ear."

"How would you describe your clientele at the store?"

Nodding, Paolucci seemed ready for the question. "At first, it was mostly people of all kinds from the neighborhood, families, widows, even some children who came in with money and lists of items from their parents. But in more recent times, there have been some new people, almost all of them men, who come in and say almost nothing."

"Do they make purchases?" Wolfe asked.

"Yes, but it is very strange. They point at items on my shelves that they want to buy, but almost none of them ever speak."

"Do you feel they are displaced persons? I have been told by Mr. Goodwin and others that there are many such individuals living in the building across the street from your establishment."

Paolucci frowned. "They are perhaps displaced persons, at least some of them. But I have to feel that many are here without the proper papers. They seem secretive and unfriendly, and they refuse to utter even a single word to me. I get a very bad feeling when many of these people come into the store."

"And you say they are almost all men?"

"Yes, Mr. Wolfe. I would say their ages are anywhere between perhaps late twenties and possibly fifty or older."

"How many would you estimate to be in this group of mysterious men?"

"At least a dozen, although it seems like I am seeing new ones every week."

"I realize these men speak very little, but do you have any idea of the nationalities they represent?"

Paolucci looked at the ceiling as if in thought. "I would say they seem to be northern or eastern European, perhaps Dutch, German, Austrian, Polish, Lithuanian. It is hard for me to tell, because I speak only Italian and English."

"Any Italians among them?" Wolfe asked.

"No, no, not at all. This of course I would know."

"Have any of these people ever threatened you?"

"No, never," Paolucci said. "But they give me an uneasy feeling that I cannot put my, how is it . . . *finger*, on. None of them ever smile, even though I welcome them, along with everyone else, with my own smile when they come into the store."

"Have these men said anything at all to you?" Wolfe asked.

"Almost never. Once a few weeks ago, one of them came in and asked in a very low, slow voice if I had a certain breakfast cereal, which I do not carry on my shelves. I could not tell what kind of accent he had. But otherwise, as I said before, not one of them has spoken to me, although they do whisper to one another very quietly, as though they are telling secrets."

"Perhaps because they are so new here, they do not know English or are embarrassed by their accents," I offered.

Paolucci dismissed my comment with the wave of a hand. "If they expect to be accepted here, they should be working hard to learn the language of this country. That is what I did, and I believe that is what all visitors should be doing as well, even the displaced persons."

"Have you ever been in the bar called McCready's?" Wolfe asked.

He shook his head. "No, never. From what I have heard, it is not such a pleasant place. Besides, whatever drinking I do is in my home. Except right now, of course," he added with a smile, indicating the glass of chianti in his hand.

"Has the bar's owner, Liam McCready, ever shopped in your store?"

"No, Mr. Wolfe. I would have recognized him, because I have seen him out on the street. He talks loudly."

"Sir, thank you for your time," Wolfe said, then turned to me. "Archie, please give Mr. Paolucci one hundred dollars from the cash drawer." I started to tell him that the grocer already had received that same amount from Saul but then realized Wolfe was aware of that and had decided to double the payment. I did as instructed, handing the money to Paolucci, whose expression was a tacit thank-you.

As Saul and I walked the one-time Italian resident down the hall, he said, "I hope that what I said was of help to Mr. Wolfe. He seems very interested in what is happening in our neighborhood—and so am I."

"I am sure he appreciates what you have told him, Mr. Paolucci," Saul put in.

"I have of course noticed that you appear to have been wounded recently, Mr. Goodwin. Does that have anything to do with Mr. Wolfe's involvement in the Elmont and its residents?"

"You are most perceptive," I told Paolucci. "If you happen to learn any more about the people you are suspicious of, I hope you telephone us." I handed him my business card and watched as he and Saul walked down the front steps of the brownstone and went off, likely in search of a taxi.

Back in the office, I dropped into my desk chair and swiveled to face Wolfe. "Well, what do you think of our immigrant shopkeeper?"

"I am impressed with his fortitude and his persistence," he said. "No doubt Mr. Paolucci has overcome numerous obstacles since his arrival in this country that he did not bother mentioning to us. Those coming here from abroad face difficulties that we who take our citizenship for granted cannot begin to imagine, including harassment, bigotry, and discrimination in the job and housing markets."

"A handsome speech. Do you feel that group in the Elmont find themselves facing the same struggles Enzo Paolucci did?"

Wolfe drank beer and set his glass down, licking his lips. "These men seem to present an altogether different set of circumstances."

"Do you care to go into detail?"

"Not at present," he said, burying himself in a book of color photographs of exotic animals. I had been dismissed.

CHAPTER 24

The next morning, as I sat in the office with coffee after breakfast, the phone rang. It was Doc Vollmer.

"Just calling to tell you and Nero Wolfe once again that there has been no change in Theodore Horstmann's condition."

"Are you optimistic or pessimistic?"

"I'm leaning toward optimism. I believe there's an excellent chance he will have a complete recovery. All of his vital signs remain positive."

"Is his sister still visiting him regularly?"

"I can't say how regularly, but almost every time I have stopped by to see him, she's been there at his bedside, looking mournful. How are you feeling, Archie?"

"Antsy, in a word. I would like to know when I can resume what I like to think of as my normal routine. I feel like the walls here are closing in around me."

"Normal for you, of course, is dashing around the city and finding trouble at every corner. You are lucky to have lived this long."

"You make my life sound more exciting than it is."

Vollmer snorted. "Why don't you stop by later this morning, say at eleven thirty, and I'll take a look at you. The concussion's effects may have worn off by now."

"It's a deal; I'll stop by." As soon as I had hung up, the phone rang again. I answered in the usual way and heard the breathless tones of the *Gazette's* Lon Cohen: "Well, there has been more trouble in Hell's Kitchen, and I'm wondering how you fit in," he said.

"It seems that you have the advantage of me."

"It's always nice to tell you something you don't know, meaning you owe me one, and which I will of course collect on at some point. Here is what we're getting off the police wire: Sometime in the early hours of this morning, Liam McCready, proprietor of the Tenth Avenue saloon bearing his name, shot and killed an intruder, who has been identified as Emil Krueger, an apparent immigrant from Germany who is here without a visa."

"Interesting. What are the cops saying?"

"Your old pal Cramer has not chosen to return our calls so far. I thought perchance you had heard from him."

"We usually hear from the inspector only when he is mad at us or thinks we have information he needs, neither of which apparently is the case here.

"For what it's worth, and probably not a lot, I chatted with McCready briefly on one of my visits to his saloon when I was trying without success to learn why Theodore Horstmann got himself beaten up and nearly killed. As I observed at the time, he fits the classic Irish mode of one filled with camaraderie and back-slapping good nature, which likely is superficial. I'm sure that you have run into the type."

"Run into the type? Hey, we've got several of them right here on our staff," Lon said. "They make damned good reporters because among other things they can charm the coins out of a Scotsman's kilt."

"Come to think of it, I have run into a few of your reporters who've got Irish roots. One of them, named Corrigan, tried to get me to sit in on a poker session with him and some of his fellow reporters from your *Gazette*. I took a pass."

"Smart move on your part. I will not say that Corrigan's game is in any way rigged, but I happen to know a few 'guests' invited to sit in who left the table with lighter wallets and vows to never return."

"Not at all like our friendly game."

"But part of the reason it's friendly is that we don't play for the kind of stakes Corrigan and his lads do," Lon put in. "Can I assume you will let me know if you happen to learn anything about that saloon shooting?"

"You know me, always ready to help."

"As you are invariably quick to say. Sometimes I think that you forget your friends, however. By the way, one of my reporters hears from a friend on the force that you were in some sort of fight in—where else—Hell's Kitchen. Care to tell me about it?"

"Not at present."

"Some friend you are. When there's news, you seem to forget me."

"Forget you—never. We will be in touch," I promised without specifying a time. When Wolfe came down at eleven, I gave him the status report on Theodore and told him about what had happened overnight at McCready's bar.

"You know nothing more than what Mr. Cohen told you?"

"No, sir, and he would like more details himself. But so far, Inspector Cramer has not responded to his calls. Want me to try Cramer?"

Wolfe's curt nod signaled me to dial a number I know well as he picked up his receiver. "Yeah?" Cramer rumbled.

"Sir, I understand there has been a fatal shooting at the McCready establishment on Tenth Avenue," Wolfe said.

"I wondered when I'd be hearing from you," the inspector said in a tired voice. "I suppose your pal from the *Gazette* filled you in."

"All we have is the bare bones, which also is all Mr. Cohen appears to possess as well."

"He's been bugging me, and I haven't had time to get back to him. I've been on the horn constantly for the last hour. You caught me between calls."

"Such is my good fortune. What can you tell Mr. Goodwin and me about what transpired in the bar?"

I could hear Cramer drawing in air and clearing his throat. "We got a report from a patrol car at . . . two forty-five this morning that a passerby walking a dog on Tenth Avenue heard a gunshot coming from inside the saloon. When our men arrived, Liam McCready was waiting for them. He said he had closed the place and turned out the lights at the usual time—they've got a two a.m. license—and he was as usual doing paperwork and counting the day's take in his small office in the back.

"He said he heard noises out in the bar area and went to investigate, taking a revolver that he keeps in his desk. He said the intruder, identified as Emil Krueger, was silhouetted against the light coming through the front window and raised his own gun as if to fire. McCready says that he shot in self-defense."

"Is Mr. McCready being held?'

"We've got him in for questioning right now, although no charges have been filed."

"What has been learned about the dead man?" Wolfe asked.

"Named Emil Krueger, last address Munich, Germany, and age forty-two, according to what few papers he was carrying. He apparently was a DP, and the chances are strong that he got over here illegally, like so many others from Europe. He wasn't carrying a visa or anything else to indicate he had passed through immigration.

"A key was found in his pocket," Cramer continued, "and it was traced—no surprise—to that Elmont building. Bauer, the super, confirmed that Krueger had been living there for about six months and was quiet, kept to himself, was well behaved, and apparently unemployed.

"Two of our men searched Krueger's quarters at the Elmont, but found nothing else of interest."

"What does the bar owner have to say for himself?"

"Rowcliff and Stebbins are questioning him right now. He doesn't have a record, and his saloon hasn't been a problem spot for the police. Do you have any thoughts?"

"None that would be of help here," Wolfe said. "What about the other man you are holding, William Hartz?"

"He is still as mute as that speak-no-evil monkey. I've told Rowcliff to see if our tavern keeper might have some thoughts on Hartz and his enforced silence. It seems like everybody knows everybody else along that block of Tenth Avenue. Anyway, you now know pretty much everything I do. I'm going to sit and pull my hair out for a while."

"The life of an inspector is not a happy one," I said to Wolfe after the call had ended.

"He is not to be envied," Wolfe agreed as I took my leave and walked down the block to Doc Vollmer's office to have my head examined—literally.

CHAPTER 25

The good news was that Vollmer declared me concussion free after putting me through several tests. The bad news: Caroline was on vacation, replaced by a dour woman of a certain age who kept looking at me and shaking her head as if I were somehow beyond hope.

I asked the doc if my recovery was unusually fast, and his reply: "I've seen all sorts of concussions over the years, some of them—like Theodore Horstmann's—extremely serious. Yours, it seems, was remarkably mild, which is your good fortune. I just hope that you take this as an omen and try not to place yourself in such risky situations. But then, I'm afraid I know you all too well."

I thanked him and walked the half-block home to find that Wolfe was not in the office, which meant he probably was in the kitchen with Fritz, consulting on—or arguing over—upcoming meals. I had just gotten seated at my desk when Saul Panzer called. "I didn't want you to think I had forgotten my assign-ments. One of them was to talk to Charlie King over at the Cabot and Sons pier. This I have done."

"And. . . ?"

"And he still suspects that his along-the-river neighbors at the National Export Lines have been smuggling DPs into New York on their ships. He told me that since you alerted him, he's seen too many strange faces coming from that pier, faces—and physiques—that definitely are not those of longshoremen. 'I know just about everybody who works over at National,' Charlie told me, 'and these are definitely not dockworkers. Hell, most of them aren't beefy enough to qualify for that kind of work. Some of them look undernourished.'

"When I asked him who he was suspicious of over at National Export, he singled out one man, Doug Halliwell, who has been the crew boss there for years. Actually, according to Charlie, Halliwell is really a lot more than crew boss. He practi-cally runs the show because the general manager and principal owner, an old guy named Chambers, spends most of the year in Palm Beach and by choice has nothing to do with the day-to-day operations on the dock. As long as the revenues are good, Chambers leaves Halliwell alone."

"What makes Charlie suspicious of Halliwell?"

"He says it's just a feeling he has about the man, nothing concrete."

"Do you know Halliwell?"

"I've met him, that's about all," Saul said. "He's tall, has a crew cut, and throws his weight around. From what Charlie has told me, his dockworkers don't care much for him, maybe because he keeps them in line like he's a Marine drill sergeant. And because a lot of these longshoremen served during the war, the last person they want to report to is somebody like that."

"Other than what he's observed, has King heard any rumors about DPs coming in on those freighters?"

"Only speculation, including among his own men, one of whom goes into McCready's on occasion and says he has seen a couple of what he refers to as 'those weird characters' in the bar who were seen getting off National Export Line ships."

"Not a lot to go on," I said.

"True, other than it would seem to confirm that the export company is a conduit for smuggling displaced persons into the United States."

"Can you think of any way we can learn more about this Halliwell character?"

"You know Del Bascom, of course."

"Of course. He was my first boss when I moved to New York, and he's worked with Wolfe and me a number of times over the years. A solid detective—and a pretty fair poker player as well."

"Well, he's had more experience on the North River docks than any other P.I. that I can think of. At least two shipping companies have used him and his agency to track down thefts off their ships, an all-too-common event. He may be able to do some sleuthing for you."

"Now that you mention it, I recall that Del has had several cases involving the docks. I will talk to my boss about it, thanks."

When Wolfe got to the office after whatever he was doing in the kitchen, I filled him in on my visit to Vollmer, Charlie King's suspicions about Doug Halliwell of National Export, and Saul's suggestion involving Del Bascom. After uncapping one of the beers Fritz had brought in, he leaned back as if in thought, presumably digesting both the beer and what I had told him.

"I am happy you appear to have recovered," he said after a two-minute silence. "As far as the suggestion that Mr. Bascom do some investigating of the National Export dock activities, are you concerned with his safety?"

"Should I be? Del knows how to take care of himself."

"Really, Archie! After what has befallen Theodore, you, and Chester Miller, caution is in order. Besides, Mr. Bascom has his own agency to run. Why should he be willing to work for me?"

"Ah, of course, what was I thinking? We don't have a client, and we would have to pay Del out of our own funds."

"Our own funds are more than adequate. That is not what troubles me, it is Mr. Bascom's well-being. You said yourself just last week that we are in better financial shape than we have been in years."

"That is true; after the fat payments we got from the Curtis blackmailing case and that Zellman insurance fraud, our bank account is healthier than this year's Kentucky Derby winning horse."

"As far as not having a client, that does not concern me in the least. In a sense, Theodore is our client, along with his sister, of course. We will do whatever it takes to discover the cause of the attack upon him and among others, yourself. Not to mention, what and who is behind the activities at the tavern, that apartment building, and the National Export dock."

"But you are against asking Bascom for help?"

Wolfe drew in a bushel of air and exhaled slowly. "Not necessarily. Telephone him."

I knew the Bascom Detective Agency number, like many others, by heart, and I dialed it. "Archie, how the hell are you?" Del boomed into the receiver. "I heard from the boys at last week's poker game that you had gotten roughed up, which is an occupational hazard. What's the story?"

"I'm much better now, and I'll fill you in on what happened eventually, but first, Nero Wolfe wants to talk to you."

"Hello, Mr. Bascom, I trust you are well."

"Not bad. Business is so-so, but it could always be better, of course. I'm not complaining, though."

"Would you be open to an assignment?"

"I might. What do you have in mind?"

"I understand you have familiarity with the goings-on at various of the Hudson River docks."

"If you are using 'goings-on' to mean theft, deception, double-dealing, and chicanery, yeah, I guess you could say over the years I've had some interesting escapades at one pier or another along our good old North River, although nothing of late."

"'Chicanery,' a fine word," Wolfe said. "Do you have knowledge of the National Export Lines facility?"

"It has been a while," Bascom said. "Last time I had anything to do with that outfit was about three, maybe four, years ago now, when someone on their crew was suspected of helping himself to diamonds and gold from South Africa that had been shipped over from one of the North Sea ports, Rotterdam. I handled that case myself, and it wasn't all that difficult to crack. One of the longshoremen had asked to be shifted from the day to the night shift—a rare occurrence.

"I suspected the man from the start, and the second night I was lurking on the docks, I grabbed him in the act. It seemed to me at the time that the National Export straw boss should have figured out what was going on, but I have always wondered if he was in on the deal."

"The name of that straw boss?" Wolfe asked.

"Halliwell, Doug Halliwell. I've never liked the guy—he's a mean one, and treats his crews like they're a bunch of slaves. He's also arrogant and self-centered, from everything I've heard. Has a big ego."

"Mr. Bascom, because of your familiarity with the docks in general, and your experience at the National Export Lines facility in particular, would you be available to do some work for me?"

Del paused before responding. "Things are a little slower than I'd like right now, so yeah, I'd consider it."

"I would like to conduct this conversation in person, if you have no objection. Are you able to come to my home tonight, say at nine?"

"All right. Is there by any chance a beer in my future?"

"There is indeed, sir."

At nine on the button, the ruddy and solidly built Del Bascom appeared at our front door, having donned a sport coat and tie, presumably in deference to Wolfe's sartorial standards.

"Come right in," I told him. "As requested, a frosty bottle of Remmers awaits you."

"Thanks, Archie. Geez, you look like you ran into somebody who had a grudge against you."

"You should have seen the other guy—he caught a slug in the leg for his troubles. You will hear more about that in the office."

Del parked in the red leather chair, greeted Wolfe, and nodded his thanks to Fritz, who presented him with a bottle of Remmers and a chilled Pilsner glass on a tray.

"I felt the complexity of the situation was better suited to a face-to-face conversation," Wolfe told our guest before drinking beer from his own glass. "I hope you have no objection."

"None whatever," Bascom said, crossing one leg over the other. "You have my full attention."

Wolfe then proceeded to go into a lengthy discourse on the chain of events that began with Theodore's beating. He left out nothing of importance.

"A helluva tale," Del remarked when Wolfe concluded. "I've been hearing a good deal of rumors about DPs getting smuggled in one way or another, and your story would seem to confirm that. There are plenty of people in this town making money at the expense of these poor, sad victims of a war they had nothing to do with."

"Well said, sir. Have you also heard of any violence connected with any of the dealings with the displaced persons?"

"The only 'violence' I've been told about is of a financial nature," Del replied. "These new arrivals who come illegally are said to pay through the nose to get smuggled in. The situation you have described is much rougher, but I have to wonder why anyone would kill, or try to kill, people because of the smuggling of DPs. It doesn't figure."

"We are in agreement," Wolfe said. "And because of the violence that has taken place, I hesitate to suggest an assignment for you."

"What kind of assignment?"

"I want to know whatever you are able to learn about Doug Halliwell's recent activities."

Bascom grinned. "By *activities*, I assume you mean actions of, shall we say, an illicit nature?"

"Nicely put, sir. But as I said, this could very well be perilous work."

"My life has been filled with perilous work," the veteran operative said, shrugging it off. "I have been shot at several times and hit just once—fortunately only in the arm. Two thugs in East Flatbush jumped me a bunch of years back, when I was on a stakeout; one of them had a cosh that he swung at me; I took it away from him and knocked him over the head with it. The other ape I hit with a roundhouse right, breaking his jaw."

"I stipulate you know how to take care of yourself, which I have never doubted," Wolfe said. "However, I would be remiss without the warning that this is dangerous work."

"I understand, and I will report back daily, and I may on occasion need to press one of my men into service on the assignment."

"So noted," Wolfe replied. "You may keep Archie apprised of developments."

CHAPTER 26

Del phoned the next morning as I sat in the office with coffee after devouring Fritz's breakfast in the kitchen. "Just checking in, nothing substantial to report," he said. "I am in the process of renewing some old acquaintances among the longshoremen and their bosses at various North River piers."

"Seen any people you would call suspicious?"

"Not so far, although I haven't ventured over to the National Export dock yet."

"Well, be careful. As the lump on my head and the stitches can attest to, someone, or some group, is playing for keeps."

"Aye, aye, sir. And in answer to a question you probably were about to ask, I am armed."

"Good. I'll look forward to your next call."

Just after I hung up, the phone jangled again. It was Lon Cohen.

"I haven't heard from you lately," he said. "Got anything for me?"

"Sorry, nothing that you would deem printable. Have you heard anything from Cramer regarding either the zipped-lip suspect or the tavern owner?"

"Not a word. The inspector has been even more uncooperative than usual. As you of all people can appreciate, our Mr. Cramer has never been easy to deal with, but this time he has set a new record for his lack of candor with those of us whose job it is to report the news to our hundreds of thousands of readers."

"You got any idea why?"

"This is only my speculation based on what I've heard, so don't attach too much importance to it. But with all that has been going on in Hell's Kitchen, I believe Cramer is dealing with something he's never handled before."

"The inspector, stymied?"

"Maybe. One of my reporters ran into him on the sidewalk outside Centre Street a couple of days ago and said he seemed not just out-of-sorts, which is common, but also more than a little depressed."

"It's possible that his job is in jeopardy. He must be constantly under pressure from his higher-ups," I said.

"I don't think that's it, Archie. From what I hear from my pipelines into the department, which are pretty solid, the inspector is in no danger whatever of losing his job."

"Good to hear. You know damned well that Wolfe and I have had our share of disagreements with him, to say the least, but we would rather deal with him than any of the other alternatives we can think of."

"Would one of those 'alternatives' happen to be one Lieutenant George Rowcliff?"

"Bingo!"

"That wasn't just a lucky guess, of course," Lon said. "You have made it clear over the years just how you and Wolfe feel about old 'pop-eyes.' And as I've told you, everybody in the press in this town has the same opinion you both have about him.

"And it's obvious Cramer would rather that Rowcliff found employment in another department, as well, even though he has been cited for bravery on more than one occasion. Enough about him. Tell me what Wolfe thinks concerning everything that's been transpiring on the docks and along Tenth Avenue in Hell's Kitchen."

"It might surprise you to learn that the man who signs my checks keeps most of his opinions to himself. I am mainly a water boy and spear carrier."

"So you say. Just don't forget who your friends are."

"How could I? You won't let me." So endeth our conversation.

When Wolfe came down from the plant rooms at eleven, I gave him Bascom's report and also reported on Lon Cohen's observations about Inspector Cramer.

"Mr. Cramer has good reason to be concerned," he said.

"Care to elucidate upon that?" I posed. He always makes a face when I use words that are part of his vocabulary, even when I use them correctly.

"I do not," he replied.

"Look, the noble medico down the block has pronounced me fit for action, and I could use some action. I would like to—" I was interrupted by the doorbell. "Who do you suppose has come to see us?" I said, returning to the office after a glance through the one-way glass on the front door.

"Admit him," Wolfe muttered with a sigh.

"Nice weather we're having," I said as I swung the door open to let in Cramer. He normally replies to my greeting with a scowl and a grunt. This time, I got only silence as he lumbered by me and headed for the office at a slower-than-usual pace.

Wolfe considered the inspector, who had dropped into the red leather chair, and without pulling a cigar from the breast pocket of his suit coat, which was unusual.

"Will you have something to drink, sir? I am about to signal Fritz to bring me beer."

"Have him bring in one more," Cramer said. "I need it."

"Indeed? Are your office walls closing in on you?"

"It sure as hell feels like it."

"Have you made any progress either with Mr. Hartz or the shooting in the McCready establishment?" Wolfe asked.

"Hartz still has an advanced case of lockjaw," Cramer said. "We can't get a damn word out of him."

"Has he been charged?"

"Yes, assault with intent to kill for his attack on Goodwin. He's being assigned a public defender, although I don't know what that poor mouthpiece can do if Hartz refuses to talk."

"Have you discovered the identity of Mr. Hartz's accomplice in the assault on Archie?"

Cramer shook his head in disgust. "We have not, since, as I said, Hartz has totally clammed up. And as for what happened in the bar, Liam McCready continues to insist that he shot that DP, Krueger, in self-defense. He says the guy had become something of a regular in the bar and was often there at closing time, which meant—according to the owner—that Krueger knew McCready kept the day's take in the office until the next morning, when he took it to the bank."

"I am under the impression most major financial institutions have an overnight depository slot on the exterior of their building," Wolfe said.

"They do, but for some reason, McCready says he prefers to deal with bank employees in person. Dates back to his years in Ireland, he says, where almost all business was transacted face-to-face.

"Anyway, he claims that somehow Krueger was able to get into the joint after closing time—or maybe hid someplace inside, maybe the men's john, before McCready shuttered the place. Whatever the case, the barkeep said he heard noises while in his office, took a revolver from his desk, and went out into the darkened bar area. He said a man—whom he didn't yet realize was Krueger—was silhouetted against a background of light coming in from the street.

"McCready told us the intruder pointed a gun at him and said, 'Don't move or I'll shoot,' and he says that in self-defense he shot first, killing Krueger with a bullet to the heart."

"Are you satisfied with the bar owner's story?" Wolfe asked.

Cramer scowled. "Hard to dispute his account. When a squad car got there, they found McCready sitting on a bar stool, with Krueger sprawled on the barroom floor with a .32 caliber S and W revolver near his body. Medics came in a couple of minutes later, and they pronounced Krueger dead. Prints were taken off the pistol, and they matched those of the dead man."

"Had there been break-ins at the bar before?"

"McCready tells us that his place is pretty peaceful, and that the neighborhood overall is quiet. I would agree, at least based on the lack of police action along that stretch of Tenth Avenue. Gunplay in the area is very rare—or at least it was until recently."

"What have you been able to learn about Mr. Krueger, other than that he is forty-two years old and comes from Munich?"

"Very little," Cramer said. "My men searched his apartment at the Elmont and found almost nothing, no identification other than his name and the address of the Elmont, no photographs or other personal papers. It's almost as if he never existed."

"How was he able to get an apartment?"

"Rowcliff asked the building superintendent, Erwin Bauer, that very question and was told that 'He seemed like a very polite young man, and he had money to pay the first two months' rent.'"

"Do they not ask to see identification in that building?" Wolfe asked.

"Seems to me they should, but in the years since the war, a lot of places in town, particularly the, shall we say, less-desirable buildings, are just happy to have their apartments filled."

For another twenty minutes, Wolfe and Cramer talked, and it was one of the stranger conversations I could recall between the two. They shared their recollections of how the city had changed since the war's end, not necessarily for the better, and how they each felt that a *malaise* (Wolfe's word) had set in. Neither of them seemed the least bit optimistic, and as they went on, I began to feel they were talking in some sort of code that I was unable to break.

Finally, Cramer rose slowly and moved toward the office door. If he was not a beaten man, he certainly was one who was on the ropes. I walked him to the front door and tried to make small talk but was met with the same lack of success as when he had entered the brownstone.

"You two certainly managed to take the sun out of what is a very bright day," I said when I was back in the office. "If Cramer had been any lower, his chin would have bounced off the steps on his way out."

I got no response from Wolfe, and I was not about to press him regarding his mood or that of the sullen inspector. My job description includes many duties, but in-house morale officer is not among them. Wolfe retreated behind his latest book, and I typed up dictation from yesterday, banging as hard as I could on the keys of the solid, old Underwood.

CHAPTER 27

That afternoon, when Wolfe was upstairs playing doctor to his orchids, I got a call from Del Bascom. "Hope you haven't had to dodge any bullets," I told him.

"Nah, all is well, Archie. Thought you'd like to know I saw your friend Charlie King at the Cabot and Sons dock, and he sends his best. I bought him lunch and we talked about Doug Halliwell."

"You have my undivided attention."

"Mr. Halliwell is not the most popular individual along the North River piers. Charlie has several men on his payroll who once worked for Halliwell, and they couldn't wait to get away from National Export. They had plenty to say about him."

"Such as?"

"Such as, he's a mean son-of-a-bitch, for starters. Deckhands who now work for Charlie say he's abusive to his men and plays favorites. After work when some of the crew head for the bars,

Halliwell expects them to buy his beers, and sometimes his meals. Those that don't get stuck with the crappiest jobs."

"Is there anything else we should know about him?" I asked.

"Yeah, I've saved the best—or maybe the worst—for last, but it will sure interest you and Wolfe. It seems that Halliwell has a buddy at the National Export dock on the other side of the pond in Hamburg. This, too, comes from one of Halliwell's former crew members who's now with Cabot and Sons. The guy in Hamburg, whose name Charlie King's man does not know, works with Halliwell to smuggle DPs across the Atlantic on National Export cargo ships."

"I'll be damned, but not surprised. Is that a lucrative business?"

"King seems to think so. A lot of these poor homeless souls, who can't get visas because they're so limited, are desperate to get out of Europe, and they'll pay whatever they have got. It isn't hard to see why, given what we've been hearing about food and housing shortages over there.

"So, there's a displaced persons' smuggling channel, apparently being run by National Export, one or more of whose employees figure to be making dirty money," Bascom went on. "But there probably are other similar routes in which DPs are being smuggled into the United States as well, wouldn't you think?"

"Sure," I agreed. "Where there is a profit to be made, the low-lifes come out from under their rocks and move in for a cut of the action."

"My question is this, Archie. Wouldn't all of these DP smugglers want to keep low and peaceful profiles to avoid having their business—as dirty as it is—come to light? Yet it seems like this particular operation is full of violence: Your man Horstmann beaten nearly to death; you coming close to getting finished off yourself; and then that poor fellow Miller, whose body was found in the river."

"And there's yet another piece of violence you may not be aware of." I told Del about what had happened in McCready's bar. "Maybe it has no connection to these other incidents, or to the National Export Lines, but the dead man, name of Krueger, was a displaced person from Germany."

"I'm not a believer in coincidences, Archie."

"Both Wolfe and Cramer have said the same thing in the past, and on more than one occasion."

"I guess that puts me in good company," Del said. "The way I look at it, there has to be some other element to this smuggling operation, probably a thing of great value, like maybe gold or diamonds or old paintings by masters—anything that would be seen by some as worth killing for. I know of a case where a man in Westchester County poisoned his aged aunt to get hold of the world-class coin collection that had belonged to her late husband."

"As Wolfe has often said, 'Greed knows no boundaries.' Of the three possibilities you mentioned, I would tend to rule out artwork, which often is too large to be smuggled without being spotted. Gold and diamonds, on the other hand, can be more easily hidden. Maybe Charlie King has some insight."

"I doubt it, but I'll ask him," Del said, and we signed off.

When Wolfe came down from the plant rooms, I repeated my conversation with Bascom, and after pushing the button for beer, he leaned back, closing his eyes. I thought he was about to go into the routine where he pushes his lips in and out, in and out, which usually means he is in a trance that ends with the solution of a mystery. But I was to be disappointed.

Wolfe opened his eyes and mouthed Bascom's words, *Anything that would be seen by some as worth killing for*. And then he mouthed them again.

"Okay, here's the way I've got it figured," I told him as he popped open the first of two beers Fritz had brought in. "Somebody is using these displaced persons to smuggle goods into this country, probably things like gold and jewelry of all kinds, stuff that likely got seized from people in Europe during and after the war. After all, the DPs are being smuggled in themselves, so what better carriers of other smuggled material? You've got to admit that's one slick way around our customs people."

Wolfe looked at me and blinked, but said nothing. "Am I boring you?" I asked.

"Boring me? Not at all. I am thinking about dinner."

"Well, that's all right, then. I felt perhaps you might be interested in the case I thought we were concentrating on. I'm going to skip dinner here and see if Lily wants to go to Rusterman's and then dancing at the Churchill."

"But we're having—"

I interrupted Wolfe. "I know what Fritz is serving tonight, and I will be sad to miss it, but I am in need of some stimulation, which seems to be in short supply here."

Before Wolfe could respond, I picked up the phone and dialed Lily Rowan's number. She answered after several rings. "Escamillo, I am glad to hear from you. I have been wondering how you are."

"Recovering nicely. I realize this is very late notice, but would you care to dine with me this evening at Rusterman's and then trip the light fantastic on the dance floor at the Churchill?"

"Well, I must say this is late notice indeed, but I would be churlish if I said no to you, Escamillo. After all, it was only three weeks ago that I called you two hours before curtain time and asked you to accompany me to the opera when a lady friend of mine backed out because of a cold."

"Then that makes us even, and it's a date. I will pick you up at seven."

Lily insisted that we first have cocktails in her tenth-floor penthouse on East Sixty-Third Street. While we were consuming Gibsons, I telephoned Rusterman's and booked a table for two—normally impossible on such short notice for anyone but Nero Wolfe or someone closely associated with him.

A few words here about Rusterman's, which is on Lexington Avenue between Forty-Ninth and Fiftieth Streets. Newspaper critics generally consider it to be the city's finest restaurant, and it is owned by Marko Vukcic, Wolfe's oldest and best friend. The two grew up together in the Balkans and fought in a resistance movement that Wolfe prefers not to discuss.

Vukcic apparently was not on the premises that night, so we were greeted by Felix, one of the owner's right-hand men. "Mr. Goodwin, Miss Rowan, so good to see you both this evening," he said, executing a courtly bow. "I know that Marko will be sad that he missed you, but I will do my best to serve you in his absence."

Felix's best, of course, was better than you are likely to find from a gastronomic standpoint anywhere else in Manhattan, with the exception of a certain kitchen in a brownstone on West Thirty-Fifth Street.

"All right, Escamillo," Lily said once we were seated at a table tucked away from both foot traffic and the chatter of other diners. "We have known each other for a long time, so there is no need to be anything but frank. Something is troubling you, and I believe it is more than just that concussion you are recovering from."

"As usual, you read me like a book, my dear. Something is going on that I can't figure out." I proceeded for several minutes to tell Lily everything that had transpired in Hell's Kitchen right up to the present.

"And what does Nero Wolfe think?"

"That's something else that I can't figure out. He isn't reacting in either of the two ways he usually does when he is at a crucial point in an investigation. He normally either—"

"Pardon the interruption," Lily said, "but I believe I can finish your sentence. Mr. Wolfe either closes his eyes, goes into a trance, and pushes his lips in and out several times and presto! he has a solution, or, if he's stumped, he goes on an eating binge for several days."

"You have summed up my boss's predictable behavior nicely," I said as we were served our guinea hens, one of the house specialties. "In this case, however, he is doing nothing and seems to either have lost interest or is totally stumped."

"I find it hard to believe Mr. Wolfe would have lost interest, given what has happened to Theodore Horstmann."

"I totally agree. Maybe I am misreading him—it would not be the first time—but Inspector Cramer also is behaving strangely. The two of them were in the office, and it seemed to me they were talking in circles, maybe because I was present and they were hiding something."

"What in the world could they possibly be hiding?" Lily asked. "Do you think you're getting paranoid?"

"I doubt that, but I suppose anything's possible. After all, I did take quite a bump on the noggin."

"You still seem like the same old Archie to me, though," Lily said, placing a hand over mine. "Are we having dessert?"

"But of course. And then it's off to the Churchill. I'm in the mood to tango the night away."

"Ah, you do indeed seem to be the same old Archie, and I wouldn't have it any other way."

CHAPTER 28

By the time I got home that night, Wolfe had gone upstairs, but he had left a handwritten note on my desk:

AG
    Please see me in my room in the morning.
NW

It isn't often Wolfe allows his morning meal to be interrupted, so I figured he was stirring himself to action. The next day after finishing my own breakfast in the kitchen, I went upstairs at seven-thirty, knocked on his bedroom door, and stepped in after hearing a muttered "enter."

As often as I have seen my boss at this early hour, I still marvel at the spectacle of him, clad in yellow pajamas in a bed covered by a black silk coverlet, and eating off a tray with folding legs. His meal was the same as mine had been: orange juice, eggs *au beurre noir*, bacon, hashed brown potatoes, and blueberry muffins. One difference: Where my morning beverage of choice is coffee, his taste runs to hot chocolate.

"Reporting as requested," I told him.

"Sit," he ordered, pointing to a bedside chair. I sat.

"I gather from your recent behavior that you do not feel I have been vigorous enough in pursuing this enigma," he said as he polished off a muffin.

"I'm frustrated that we don't seem to be getting anywhere."

"Frustration often leads to impulsive and unwise actions," Wolfe replied. "Do you have any suggestions?"

"Not right now," I said. "I was hoping you had some sort of plan."

He drew in air and let it out slowly. "It has been nearly a year since Mr. Cohen has eaten with us," he said.

"That's correct—last August, to be exact."

"Invite him to dine here tonight. Tell him we are having *vitello tonnato* along with broccoli and herb-stuffed potatoes."

"Shall I also mention an after-dinner snifter of Remisier is included in the menu?"

"Not necessary. Mr. Cohen knows that the elixir is always available on his visits."

I wasn't sure having Lon Cohen over for dinner was a sign Wolfe was going back to work, but I was all for it. When I phoned him, Lon sounded harried, as usual, but he had time to say, "Nice to hear from you, of all people. Have you called with something I can use on page one tomorrow?"

"No, I—"

"Then I'm not interested. You have not exactly been forthcoming lately, so—"

"Now it's my turn to do the interrupting, dammit. Nero Wolfe would like you to join us for dinner tonight."

That brought him up short. "Dinner at the brownstone? I never say no to that invitation. Although I suppose I am expected to sing for my supper."

"My boss didn't say. You can always claim you have another engagement."

"Not a chance. I will be there, with shoes shined and wearing a fresh shirt."

"What more can we ask for?"

At six thirty, I answered the doorbell and admitted Lon Cohen, who was indeed presentable. Wolfe had not yet come down from his room, so I mixed drinks for Lon and me and we sat in the office. "I hope your boss isn't expecting a lot from me," he said. "By the way, you look kind of funny, with some of your hair shaved off. You never have told me what happened to you, and all I have to go by is police gossip from one of our reporters."

"It's a long story," I told him, "and it will probably come out later tonight."

When Wolfe did make his appearance, we went into the dining room, where we were served the *vitello tonnato*, which, for those of you like me not conversant with Italian, is a dish consisting of veal and tuna. In Fritz's hands, it was delicious.

Lon knew our protocol enough to realize business is not discussed during meals, and he also knew Wolfe invariably selected the subject for dinner table discussion. This night it was the Marshall Plan, which had been instituted in 1948 by the United States to give financial aid to Western European countries that had been devastated by World War II. Lon was enthusiastic over the success of the plan, Wolfe less so, feeling certain countries were favored over others in the doling out of the dollars—millions of them. As usual, I took a neutral position.

In the office with coffee after dinner and dessert, Lon settled into the red leather chair, savoring that snifter of Remisier he knew would be coming his way, as was always the case on his visits. "As pleasant as this evening has been, I have a feeling I was invited for a reason," he said to Wolfe, running a hand over his dark, slicked-back hair.

"Mr. Cohen, this is a question I have often posed: Would you say that on balance, are we more or less even, involving favors we have bestowed upon each other?"

"I would agree. I feed you information, and you feed me what turn out to be scoops. Overall, it has worked out on both sides."

"Very well. You have of course noticed that Archie shows signs of physical strife, and we will go into that in the course of the evening. First, a question. Have your reporters encountered many cases of smuggling, particularly involving displaced persons who are in this country either legally or otherwise?"

Lon took a sip of the cognac, savored it, and exhaled. "If there has been a lot of smuggling on the part of the incoming DPs, our men haven't picked up on it. And neither, as far as we are aware, have the police or the immigration authorities. Oh, no doubt some of these people have brought things in on a small scale that they, shall we say . . . 'borrowed' from others in Europe before they left."

"Do you have any sense of what percentage of the displaced persons who have entered this country since the end of the war are here without documentation?" Wolfe asked.

The newspaperman sighed and turned his palms upward. "I'm not sure anyone has a definitive answer to that. For as much as the government likes to claim how strict we are in allowing people into this country, the truth is that our borders really are a sieve. I am convinced that there are uncounted numbers of aliens on the streets of this city right now. We figure many of them were brought over by family members who paid somebody to get them here using phony or stolen identification papers."

"It appears to be a furtive and burgeoning industry."

"That's a good way to phrase it," Lon said. "And that so-called industry is damned near impossible to penetrate. At the risk of using a cliché, there's a conspiracy of silence. And it seems to us at the *Gazette* that a lot of government officials are looking the other way, maybe because they feel it's fruitless to try prying information out of the people responsible for bringing their relatives or friends across from Europe."

"Clans invariably close their ranks," Wolfe remarked. "Some of what I am about to relate, you already know, but I feel you merit transparency from Archie and me."

With that, Wolfe launched into a detailed recitation of all that had transpired since the attack of Fritz. He left nothing out, including my run-in with those two men and my subsequent shooting of one of them, William Hartz.

"Oh yeah, we know about Hartz. He's clammed up, right?"

"As far as we know," I put in. "He was assigned a public defender who, last we heard, had not been able to get him to open his yap at all."

"Have there been any further developments in that tavern shooting?" Wolfe asked.

"Nothing we've heard of," Lon said. "The cops are still calling it self-defense on the part of the bar owner."

"Do you have anything to add to what I have summarized, Mr. Cohen?"

"Not really. We are at a dead end on the whole business. I was hoping you might have some words of wisdom."

"Wisdom seems to be in short supply at the moment," Wolfe said. "Has your network of reporters and their sources noticed any spike in smuggling activities involving valuable merchandise?"

"No, and believe me, we have been looking. Our 'sources,' as you term them, are well plugged into the world of fences and other intermediaries who trade in that quaint old phrase, 'ill-gotten goods.' The only recent example I can think of is when a couple of months back, three pieces of priceless Renaissance artwork were discovered in the back room of a small Greenwich Village gallery, thanks to a tip we received. You may have read our article that ran at the time."

"I did," Wolfe said, uncapping a frosted bottle of beer that Fritz had brought in. "But I find it hard to believe that is the only example to have been discovered."

Lon nodded. "I concur, which may indicate the degree of secrecy with which smugglers operate. I have no doubt that other examples of this kind will eventually come to light. In the meantime, though, the single most prevalent element secretly coming into this country is not riches but people, which can be viewed as both good and bad."

Wolfe leaned back in his chair and stared straight ahead, apparently oblivious to us. Lon looked at me, his face registering puzzlement, and I rolled my eyes. Our guest drained the last of his Remisier and rose. "Time for me to be off. Thanks for the dinner, the conversation, and this," he told Wolfe, holding up the empty snifter in a salute. He got no response and sent another puzzled expression in my direction as he rose to leave.

When I walked Lon down the hall to the door, he said, "It seems like your boss is in a trance. Was it something I said?"

"Beats me. I think I've told you that when he is in the middle of a case, he often closes his eyes and pushes his lips in and out, which means he's working on a solution, which in itself is a sort of trance. But this . . . I've never seen it before."

"Do you think he's all right?"

"We will know soon enough," I said as Lon went down the steps of the brownstone, shaking his head and striding off in search of a cab.

When I got back to the office, Wolfe was gone. Thinking he went to consult with Fritz about tomorrow's meals, I went to the kitchen, but he wasn't there. "Mr. Wolfe must have gone to bed, Archie," I was told by our chef. Okay, the resident brain is in some sort of mood that I can't quite read, but I am not going to worry about it until tomorrow, I told myself, as I headed upstairs to get my requisite 510 minutes of sleep.

CHAPTER 29

Before I fell asleep, a plan began to take root in my brain, a plan that would need Wolfe's approval.

When I rose the next morning, the first thing I did was to look myself over in the mirror. I definitely felt I was presentable. The bruises had gradually faded, although my hair was slow in growing back in the area where I'd been sutured. But a visit to my barber, Calvin, could help to camouflage the temporary violence that had been done to my scalp.

I showered, shaved, and dressed, but instead of going straight to the kitchen for breakfast as usual, I went down one flight and knocked on Wolfe's bedroom door.

"Yes?"

"It's me, Archie. I need to see you."

The response was a grunt. "You know very well I am eating."

"This can't wait."

Another grunt. "Enter!"

Wolfe had nearly polished off the food on his tray, so I didn't feel as though I had interrupted his breakfast, although his expression made it clear he was not happy to see me. "Well?" he demanded.

"I have an idea of how to move things along, and I felt I should get your approval." I then went on to lay out my plan as Wolfe drained the last of his cup of hot chocolate. When I was done, his face was stony. "I don't like it," he said.

"Why not?"

"You have been through a great deal already. This could place you in further peril without substantially aiding our cause."

"With respect, I believe what I have proposed might break the logjam we seem to find ourselves stuck in."

Wolfe seemed unmoved, but I continued to press him. I often have called him stubborn over the years, but he is well aware that I can be just as mulish as he. We continued to spar for several more minutes, and I could sense that I was wearing him down. Finally, he said, "All right, confound it, begin your preparations, and we will talk later today."

This was a victory of sorts. After my own breakfast, I called Calvin the barber and was able to get a nine-thirty appointment. "I need to play down this spot where I had to get my head shaved because of a cut," I told him when I entered his two-man shop on Lexington. "What do you think?"

"One way is to give you a closer overall cut than usual, Archie. Do you see that as a problem?"

"Just don't make me look like a buck private in boot camp."

Calvin laughed. "Give me a little credit. I think I can do this so that no one will notice. It may take a little getting used to, but I'm sure you can handle it."

"Do your worst—or rather, your best," I told him. And when he was done, I had to admit that I looked presentable, at least to those who didn't know me. And my plan was to meet someone who had never seen me before.

After leaving the barbershop, I went to a small-job printing operation on Madison Avenue that we had patronized in the past. The owner, Larry Berg, greeted me as I walked into his shop. "Archie Goodwin, of all people! You haven't been around for many moons. Let me guess: You want business cards that make you a . . . what? Stock broker? Used car salesman? Crane operator? Black jack dealer?"

"Nice try, Larry. Over the years, your cards have made me into a number of other people, and in my work, those cards have come in handy. Today, here is what I want . . ."

I left the print shop less than a half hour later with a batch of handsomely printed and authentic-looking business cards. I was setting out on a new career, if only briefly.

My next stop was in the theater district, specifically "Broadway Costumery & Small Props," a windowless street-level shop on West Forty-Fourth Street next door to a playhouse that was staging a first-run musical. I stepped in to the sound of a tinkling bell over the door.

"Yes, sir, may I help you?" asked a small and slender man with slicked-down hair and wearing a yellow ascot and a bright blue sports coat. "My name is Will, as in Shakespeare."

"I'm looking for some eyeglasses," I told him.

"With plain lenses, of course," he replied.

"Of course. Is this a popular request?"

"Oh my, yes. Some, shall we say . . . *older* performers of my vintage tend to sport faux glasses because they cover what we might describe as facial imperfections."

"Such as wrinkles or bags under the eyes, you mean?"

"Well, that's true, although I try to avoid using those words when dealing with my customers. Of course, there are other reasons for wearing glasses while onstage. Perhaps a performer is playing the role of a college professor or a scientist. Or in the case of a woman, a schoolteacher. Glasses can provide what we refer to as 'gravitas.'"

"Gravitas is important," I said. "I'm looking for a pair that will make me appear serious."

"Are you currently performing?"

"No, at least not in the theater."

"So, I gather you are not a member of Actors' Equity," the proprietor said. When I shook my head, he added, "I always ask, because we give Equity members a five percent discount on any purchases. I didn't think you were an actor in the classical sense. You seem to me more like a private investigator or possibly someone in the repossession business."

I replied with a smile, nothing more, and after an awkward silence, the shop's owner, if that's what he was, turned to shelves behind him and pulled out several trays, which he laid on the counter. "Here is our selection," he said with pride.

They were all sizes and colors—old-lady glasses, sunglasses of many hues, horned rims, monocles, rimless models, pince-nez that clipped to the nose. "I think this is exactly what I'm looking for," I told the man, pointing to a pair of the horned rims.

"Good choice," he said like a good salesman. "Put them on and take a look in the mirror."

I looked different, neither better or worse than before, just different. "Would you like to try on some others?" Will asked.

"No, these should do nicely."

He quoted me a price and I handed him the cash. When I turned to go, the man behind the counter said, "Whatever line you are in, be sure to tell your friends and colleagues about us. We are here for everyone, whatever their profession, and we of course have a wide variety of clothes, hats, even shoes."

I told him that I would spread the word, and as I started to leave, a thirtyish platinum blonde woman, hair stacked high atop her head and with a heavily made-up face and plenty of curves, entered and rewarded me with a wink for holding the door for her. I winked back, wondering who she was playing and what she needed in the way of a costume to enhance her role. I would never know.

When I returned to the brownstone, I put on the glasses and walked into the kitchen. "How do I look?" I asked Fritz.

He looked up from stirring something in a pan and blinked. "I did not realize you need glasses, Archie."

"I don't, I'm going undercover." That brought a frown from Fritz, who already had expressed his concern over what had happened to me earlier.

"What will Mr. Wolfe say when he sees you?"

"We'll find out at eleven. I have become a new man, Fritz."

"No, you're the same old Archie," he said, turning back to his stirring.

"Thanks a lot," I said, returning to the office.

CHAPTER 30

I was reading the just-delivered *Gazette* when Wolfe, fresh from the plant rooms, strode into the office. I looked up at him and smiled.

"So, you have done it," he said as he sat at his desk.

"Yep, what do you think? Do I look professional?"

"You look . . . different."

"Well, that's the idea, isn't it?" I said, swiveling to face him. "Between the glasses and the shorter hair, I hope to seem like a different person with, of course, a different name." I tossed one of my new business cards onto his desk.

He looked at it with a frown. "*5 Boroughs Magazine.* Who conceived that title?"

"I did, who else? A great name for a new local publication, don't you think?"

His response was to begin going through the mail I had stacked on his blotter.

After lunch, undaunted by Wolfe's lukewarm reaction to my transformation, and my new "employer," I left the brownstone with a reporter's notebook I had cadged from Lon Cohen years ago. My destination: The North River.

The National Export Lines dock was quiet when I stepped onto it. One ship, with a Swedish name and blue-and-yellow flags, was moored, but nothing seemed to be going on.

"Can I help you, mate?" a bearded longshoreman asked.

"I am looking for Mr. Douglas Halliwell," I told him.

"In his office, halfway toward the river," he said, pointing in a westerly direction.

The small office, which looked a lot like Charlie King's over at the Cabot & Sons pier, was cluttered with stacks of papers. At a small desk amid the clutter, a muscled man with a crew cut was hunched over, writing in what appeared to be a logbook or a ledger. "Mr. Halliwell?" I asked.

"Yeah, whaddya want?" he said, looking up at me through bloodshot eyes.

"My name is Stuart Moore, and I'm a writer for a brand-new local publication, *5 Boroughs Magazine*," I told him, placing my card, complete with the periodical's artistic logo designed by me and Larry Berg, in front of him. "For our very first issue, we are doing profiles of some of the people who make this great city work. Your name was one of the first suggested to us, and of course New York's role as a great port must be represented in our article."

"Who suggested me?'

"Someone from the Port Authority, I forget his name. But he told us that you run one of the biggest and best operations along the North River."

"That so?" Halliwell said, his unshaven face creased with a smile. "Well, I've been at it for a long time, and I guess you could say that I know my way around this river and this harbor."

"Do you mind if I take a few minutes of your valuable time?"

"Uh, okay . . . sure. What can I tell you for your story?" Halliwell's mood had quickly gone from sour to downright amiable. I could see that what had been told about his having a big ego worked in my favor.

"First off, because this is a profile, our readers will be anxious to know how you got into this business in the first place."

Halliwell, who did not ask me to sit down, leaned back in his chair and clasped his hands behind his head, as if deep in thought. "When I was eighteen and had just graduated from high school in Queens, I needed to get a job. My father, who was a welder, happened to know a guy who worked on the docks over in Brooklyn, his name was Morrissey. He managed to use his influence, to get me on a crew. So I guess you could say that I landed my first full-time job through connections, but—are you writing all this down?—I soon showed that I was very capable, and before long, I was doing more heavy labor than most of the veteran hands on the dock."

"Very impressive," I said, making a show of scribbling in my notebook. "You must have worked during the Depression."

"Oh, I did, and that's when I moved up through the ranks, you might say. I eventually left Brooklyn and came over here, to this very dock. At the time, Mr. Chambers, who is still the principal owner and general manager of National Export, wanted to cut back and spend more time in Florida. He increasingly gave me added responsibilities, and now he pretty much lets me run this operation."

"That is quite a success story," I said. More scribbling.

"Well, Sam—Mr. Chambers, that is—knows that he can trust me," Halliwell said, clearing his throat.

"What happened when we went to war?"

"I enlisted, of course. Who wouldn't?" he said, sitting up straighter and squaring his shoulders. "You look to be the right age. I assume you served."

"Yes, for three years. Did you see action?"

"I was with the army in Germany and have the medals to prove it," he said, trying without success to sound casual. "It was frustrating, I'll tell you. We didn't get to Berlin in time to keep the Russkies out, and now look at the mess we've got: The lousy Commies elbowed their way in. If only we had supported those tough Krauts longer instead of destroying their army, then they could have held the damned Reds at bay at least long enough for us to block their entry into Berlin. Eastern Europe wouldn't be in such a mess and Berlin wouldn't have gotten carved up like it is. And also, we wouldn't have had to use that damned airlift.

"It was obvious to us over there at the time that the Germans weren't our real enemies, it was Stalin and that Moscow bunch," Halliwell went on. "I'm sure in whatever your role was, you were aware of that too."

I made no comment, saying, "I gather that when the war was over, you got your old job back here at National Export."

"Sam Chambers held the fort while I was in uniform, and, boy, was he glad to see me come back. The biggest smile I've ever seen was when he turned things back over to me and made a beeline for Palm Beach."

"So, he continues to be happy with the way you run this pier?"

"That's what he tells me every time we talk on the phone. Revenues are up, and the crew here are doing their job."

"It sounds like you work well with your men."

"Mr., what is it . . . Moore?" Halliwell said, looking at my business card, "I have always tried to run this operation in an organized way. And since returning from military service, I've become more conscious than ever of the importance of a strict chain of command."

"Were you an officer?"

"No, but I had plenty of authority as a Sergeant First Class, and if the fighting had gone on much longer, I was in line to become a First Sergeant. What about you, Mr. Moore?"

"Because of the nature of my assignment, I'm afraid even now that I am not allowed to discuss my rank or where I served."

Halliwell nodded. "Understood. Intelligence work, eh?"

It was my turn to nod. "I'm sure that your crew members here respect you."

"They do, I can guarantee that."

"I assume most of the ships you load and unload are from foreign ports, right?"

"Yes. Of course, New York has one of the great harbors in the world, but I guess I don't have to tell you that. It's part of the reason your magazine is doing this story."

"Do you have any interesting experiences to relate about the type of merchandise you receive from overseas?"

Halliwell scratched his head. "I can't think of any funny stories, if that's what you mean. Right now, we're sending more things to Europe than we're getting from them, because they're still in the long process of rebuilding."

"What about smuggling? Do you run into much of that?"

He jerked upright in his chair. "Smuggling—no!" He seemed shocked that I would even raise the topic.

"I just wondered, because over the years there have been stories of artwork and watches and gold and other valuable items finding there way here, especially from Europe."

"Well, we haven't had any—yeah, what is it?" Halliwell swiveled as one of his longshoremen knocked on the glass of his door and opened it a crack. "I need to see you, Chief," he said.

"I'll be right back," Halliwell said, getting up, going outside, and closing the door behind him. He and the dockworker walked several paces away from the office, and I could hear the muffled sound of loud words, most of them delivered by the boss. He came back in, running a hand over his forehead. He had no long hair to smooth. "Sorry, there's been a little disagreement, and I'll have to settle it, but that can wait. Do you have any more questions for me?"

"I don't think so. We'd like to get a photograph, of course. Can I send someone here to take a shot of you on the pier?"

"Tell you what," Halliwell said, "I just happen to have picture that I'm sure would work. I'd really rather not have someone come here with a camera. I think it looks bad for the men to see their superior being photographed like some sort of a big shot." He went to a filing cabinet and pulled out a black-and-white glossy of him on the dock, hands in his pockets, squinting up at a freighter and wearing a thoughtful expression. "Will this do?"

"I'll show this to my editor and see what he thinks," I said as I left the office. "The pier doesn't seem busy right now."

"Yeah, this happens sometimes. We're supposed to be getting a ship in later today from Rotterdam. As you know, that port was heavily bombed during the war, and only in the last year or so is it getting back to where it was before 1939."

"It has taken all of Europe a long time to recover, and they are not there yet." I observed.

"And the Commies sure aren't helping much," Halliwell said. "Make sure I get a copy of your magazine when it comes out."

I told him I would and walked off the pier, happy I had encountered so few longshoremen. Although if I had run into any who had seen me in McCready's, I doubt they would have recognized me in my bespectacled get-up.

CHAPTER 31

Rather than returning to the brownstone after I left the National Export dock, I called Fritz and told him I wouldn't be around for lunch. "It's nothing personal," I told him, "I just have some things I need to do." Then, feeling very much like a martyr for missing a wonderful meal, I grabbed a ham sandwich and a glass of milk in a little café on Ninth Avenue that I had frequented in the past. And lest you think I was overly denying myself the good life, I chased my sandwich with a wedge of apple pie—à la mode.

The reason I didn't go home after talking to Halliwell was that I wanted to process our interview, and the best way for me to do that was to be alone. I continued my processing after the meal by walking at a leisurely pace as far north as Fifty-Ninth Street, where Ninth Avenue changes its name to Columbus. I then hiked back south like a man who was taking his time to enjoy a sunny June afternoon.

When I got back to the brownstone, it was just after four, meaning Wolfe would be upstairs with the orchids. Fritz heard me let myself in the front door and he arrived in the office just as I did. "Archie, Mr. Wolfe has been asking about you and requested that you telephone him in the plant rooms."

"Disturb him during his playtime? That is serious," I said, picking up the phone.

"Yes?" came his bark.

"I'm back and can report any time it's convenient for you."

"That can wait until before dinner. Call Inspector Cramer and see if he can be there tonight at nine."

"Do I give him a specific reason?"

"You do not," he said, hanging up.

Swell. Wolfe knows Cramer's number at work and is perfectly capable of dialing it himself, but why should he, since he had his very own wage slave handy?

"Cramer!" came the response after three rings. I held the phone away from my head to protect my eardrum.

"Mr. Wolfe wonders if you could pay him a visit tonight at nine p.m."

"Oh, he does, does he? And I suppose he didn't share with you his reason?"

"Correct. But as you know from experience, he usually has a good reason for his requests."

"A *request*? Is that what you call it? I've known Wolfe longer than you have, and he sees what you call a request to be more like a command."

"If you feel that way, Inspector, you are free to ignore his invitation."

"And it's possible I will do just that," Cramer said, although there was a lack of conviction in his voice. I bet myself that it was three-to-one he would show up at the brownstone that night.

When Wolfe made his descent by elevator from the plant rooms and settled into his office chair with beer, I asked why he wanted to see Cramer, but he ignored the question. "Tell me about your meeting with Mr. Halliwell."

As I always do, I repeated our conversation verbatim as Wolfe leaned back, eyes closed. When I finished, he said nothing.

"Any thoughts?" I asked.

"No. Did Mr. Cramer complain about my request?"

"Of course he did, which shouldn't surprise you. But I got the distinct impression that he will be here."

At 8:55 p.m., the doorbell rang. "Now who do you suppose that is?" I asked Wolfe, who didn't bother to look up from a magazine he had been frowning at.

I went to the front door and swung it open, admitting for at least the five-hundredth time Inspector Cramer of the Homicide Squad. "And a good evening to you, sir," I said, getting a grunt in reply as he tromped down the hall to the office, where as usual he dropped into the red leather chair, pulling out a cigar.

"All right, dammit, I'm here, Wolfe. What—if anything— have you got to tell me?"

"Do you know what a ratline is, sir?"

Cramer jammed the unlit stogie into his mouth and frowned. "No, any reason that I should?"

"Not particularly, except the term may well be related to a series of events that have occurred recently in Hell's Kitchen."

"By events, I assume you mean Horstmann's beating, Goodwin's own beating and his shooting of one of his assailants, the killing of that man found in the river, and the fatal shooting in the bar?" Cramer ticked off each of the events on a finger as he recited them.

"Precisely."

"Now what the hell is a ratline?"

"The answer to that can wait, sir. I believe I know what has been occurring, and why."

"Are you in a mood to share your thoughts?" Cramer asked, leaning forward and leading with his jaw.

"Not at the moment. I would like to assemble some individuals in this room."

The inspector took a deep breath, and his exhale made a whistling sound. "I knew this would eventually come," he said. "There will be no assembling here."

"Meaning?" Wolfe replied, eyebrows raised.

"Meaning that the commissioner does not want any more of what I call your 'séances' in this house. He says that it's bad for the department's reputation to have a private investigator do our work for us."

"Really? In the past, we—Archie and I—have gone to great lengths to ensure that the department—and by extension, you—receive full credit for the results of an investigation we have undertaken together."

"I know, I know," Cramer said, running a hand through his thinning salt-and-pepper hair. "But as you are only too well aware, word has gotten out about what goes on here."

"It was that damned feature in the *Herald Tribune* about us several months ago," I said. "Mr. Wolfe and I wouldn't talk to the reporter, but he already had got an account from a woman who was one of the people in this room when the murderer of that pawn shop owner confessed. And then she gave the *Tribune* guy the names of two others who were there at the time, and the paper ended up with quite a story."

"Goodwin's right," the inspector said. "There was hell to pay at headquarters when that piece came out. I was on the carpet with the commissioner for more than an hour."

"I am sincerely sorry for what befell you, sir," Wolfe said, meaning it. "I assume you also are under pressure now for what has transpired in the Hell's Kitchen region in recent days. Many of the city's newspapers are suggesting that area is the city's new 'hot spot' for violence, which must increase the heat upon you and your subordinates."

"I can't quarrel with that," Cramer said, "but the heat comes naturally with the job. I'm not complaining."

"Understood. I would like to propose a compromise that may be at least somewhat more palatable to your superiors."

"Which is?" Cramer posed warily.

"Which is that a 'séance,' to use your term, would be held in a police department facility."

"That could be a problem," the inspector said.

"Why?" Wolfe demanded.

"Red tape. I can't simply snap my fingers and commandeer a facility where you can pontificate. Besides, how do I know whom you want to invite and whom you intend to identify as a killer? I know how much you like to put on a show."

Wolfe sighed. "Very well, here is the list of individuals I would request be present." He listed them and their locations, which only slightly surprised me. If Cramer also was surprised, he did a good job of hiding it.

"You've got one tough sell here," the inspector said. "I don't like it."

"Why not?" Wolfe asked, turning his palms up.

"For one thing, how am I going to spring someone from stir to attend this . . . this session?"

"Really, Mr. Cramer, I am not requesting a prisoner be released into the outside world, but rather moved temporarily from one governmental facility to another. This is done every day as individuals are transported in a barred vehicle from a jail cell to a courtroom to stand trial."

The inspector still seemed resistant. "I would not want to hold such a session at Headquarters."

"I understand your reluctance," Wolfe said. "What about one of the precincts as a meeting place?"

"That's risky, too," Cramer said, although I could sense his reluctance was beginning to weaken.

"Surely you have built a coterie of strong supporters throughout the force—individuals who are indebted to you in one way or another."

"I do not make a practice of cashing IOUs," the inspector said stiffly.

"But you are in the business of seeing justice done," Wolfe countered. "Cashing an IOU, to use your phrase, would seem a small price to pay to discover what has been transpiring in the Hell's Kitchen neighborhood."

Despite the many verbal clashes we have had in the past, I felt sympathy for Cramer, who is without doubt a good cop. I have never envied him his position, and it seemed obvious that all of those years on the hot seat have begun to wear him down.

It also seemed obvious he was conflicted and was struggling to make a decision. Finally, he said, "The commanding officer of a precinct on the Lower East Side is a captain I worked with early in his career. He has told me more than once that I was responsible for him staying on the force when he was going through a rough time with one of his superiors. I'm not sure how much I really did for him, but . . ." He let it trail off, shrugging.

"For all the harsh words that have passed between us over the years, I have never lost sight of the fact that you are a very modest individual, sir," Wolfe said. "You prefer to not dwell upon your own accomplishments but rather on those of others, which is an admirable trait. I am sure the individual's comments are heartfelt."

"Yeah, yeah," Cramer said, waving the comment away and coloring slightly. "Anyway, this captain, named Ryan, runs a precinct that's all the way across Manhattan from Hell's Kitchen."

"It could serve our purposes," Wolfe remarked, although I could see that the inspector was still conflicted. "And if you recall, we once held what you refer to as a séance in police headquarters."*

"That was before you finally became *persona non grata* with the top brass," Cramer said.

"I can understand your reluctance to have a meeting in a police facility, but this would appear to be the best solution."

Cramer rose slowly, as if it were an effort. "I will telephone Kevin Ryan," he said without enthusiasm. "However, the last thing I want to do is put him in any kind of jeopardy with the hierarchy at 240 Centre Street."

"I am not familiar with the intricacies of the police department and its internal system of communications, so my question might seem naïve to you," Wolfe said. "Is it possible to keep word of our proposed gathering from reaching the almighty citadel on Centre Street?"

"Hell, anything's possible," the inspector said over his shoulder as he walked out of the office. "But I'll make sure that Ryan knows the score."

"Well, you've managed to put Cramer on the hot seat," I told Wolfe when I returned from seeing the inspector out.

---

* *The Battered Badge* by Robert Goldsborough (2018)

"I have no doubt he is capable of taking care of himself, Archie. He would not have lasted this long without a strong sense of self-preservation."

"I guess. Still, it seems to me we're skating on thin ice." That brought another one of the looks I get from Wolfe when he reacts to one of my figures of speech.

CHAPTER 32

The next morning when I was in the office after breakfast with coffee, the phone jangled. It was the inspector.

"I know that your boss is up with his precious, damned orchids right now, and heaven knows I am not about to disturb the man while he's playing. But you can tell him that I've arranged a meeting at that Lower East Side precinct for nine tomorrow night." He read the address.

"Now, about the people Mr. Wolfe wants in attendance. I can—"

"Never mind that, Goodwin. Remember, I got all the names from him and where to find them, and I will take care of the so-called 'invitations.' The less Wolfe has to do directly with this operation, the better. I'm the one who figures to take the fall for what may well be a fiasco, but what the hell—in for a penny, in for a pound."

"It can't be that bad, Inspector."

"Oh yes, it can. I've got to be insane for agreeing to this, and my wife agrees. But she's been after me to retire for years, so she didn't try very hard to talk me out of this. You'll be driving Wolfe to the precinct, I suppose?"

I told him, yes, that is the plan, and Cramer hung up before I could say goodbye. I contemplated calling Wolfe in the plant rooms but felt the news could wait until he came down at eleven. He made a face when I gave him the details, and I knew his reaction was not so much that he would have to exercise his brain, but that he would be forced to ride in an automobile all the way across Manhattan—and back again.

I had a vague idea what my boss was planning for the meeting tomorrow night, and I started to ask him about it when the telephone rang. "Hello, Archie," Doc Vollmer said, and I signaled Wolfe to pick up his instrument, mouthing the doctor's name.

"This is Nero Wolfe. Do you have news of Theodore?"

"I do. He has been showing slight signs of emerging from his coma, but I caution you to control your optimism. I have seen numerous cases where a patient appears to be recovering from a condition similar to Mr. Horstmann's, only to relapse."

"Has he spoken?"

"Oh no, nothing so startling as that, but he continues to indicate recognition when his sister appears—facial tics, a fluttering of the eyes, the beginnings of a smile."

"Would it be beneficial were I to visit him?" Wolfe asked.

"How would you characterize your relationship with Mr. Horstmann?" the doctor replied.

"You know very well that we have worked together for many years."

"You did not answer my question. Would you describe your association as convivial?"

"Our 'association,' to use your term, has been a professional one," Wolfe said icily.

"My suggestion would be to have Mr. Horstmann's sister continue as his sole visitor," Vollmer replied in a tone as cold as Wolfe's. The doctor had been familiar with life at the brownstone long enough to realize that Wolfe and his gardener had had their share of disagreements—some of them heated.

"Please inform me when there has been further improvement in Theodore's condition," Wolfe snapped, slamming his instrument into its cradle.

"You should be happy you don't have to visit the hospital again," I told my boss. "It's tough enough that you will have to travel all the way to the Lower East Side with a madman at the wheel of our Heron sedan."

Of course, my comment was ignored, and no words were spoken between us until dinner. Even then, the conversation was strained.

The next morning, I woke up feeling on edge, as I always do on the days when Wolfe is to stage one of his "here's who did it" events. Don't ask me why I get edgy at these times, because I can't explain it. I know it makes no sense, as invariably my boss delivers a solution. Maybe I have a subconscious concern that this will be the time he fails.

I barely spoke a word in the kitchen as I ate breakfast at my small table and read the *Times,* in which I found nothing to interest me. Fritz frowned with concern but said nothing, knowing my moods as well as Wolfe does. After breakfast, I moved to the office with coffee and puttered around, dusting the top of my desk, filing the latest set of orchid germination records that Carl Willis had brought down, and cleaning my typewriter with the little brush that came with the machine.

I then went to my room and pulled two suits out of the closet, throwing them over an arm and walking down to the kitchen, where I announced to Fritz that I was taking a walk and would be back "at an unspecified time." The dry cleaner we use is three blocks east on Thirty-Fifth Street, and being out in the summer air was refreshing and improved my mood to the degree that I almost whistled at a redhead in a green dress who smiled at me as we passed on the sidewalk. I controlled myself, though, keeping in mind a newspaper feature I had recently read warning that "women do not like men who whistle, shout, or otherwise make gestures to them on the streets that they might consider to be rude."

"Nice to see you, Archie Goodwin," said Anna Blazek, who had run the cleaners alone since her husband's death. "You have not been in for a while."

"I guess I haven't been too hard on my suits lately. How's business?"

"Good enough to keep me going, but not so good that I can retire to Florida, which, as I've told you, is my dream."

"You don't belong in Florida, you are a New Yorker through-and-through," I told her. "Besides, I would miss seeing your welcoming face behind the counter here if you were off at some beach wearing sunglasses and gazing out on blue waters."

"You say the nicest things to a girl," Anna said, batting dark eyes and letting a dimpled smile crease her broad Slavic face.

I left the shop with my spirits lifted, and although I hadn't consciously realized it when I set out, that was the real reason I took the suits in. They had not needed cleaning. That brief encounter was enough to see me through the rest of the day.

CHAPTER 33

That night after dinner and coffee in the office, I told Wolfe it was time to drive to the Lower East Side precinct. He sighed in recognition as I got up, walked through the kitchen to the back door of the brownstone, and left by the rear gate. A gangway between buildings led me to Thirty-Fourth Street and Curran Motors, where we had garaged our cars for years.

The night man, who I had not met before, gave me the keys to the Heron sedan and offered to pull the car out for me, but I told him I would handle it. Once, years ago, another Curran employee had dented a fender backing one of our cars out, and since then, no one but me has ever taken the car out of Curran's.

By the time I pulled around in front of the brownstone, Wolfe was already standing at the top of the stairs, wearing a broad-brimmed hat and carrying his bentwood walking stick. He carefully descended a step at a time, wearing the grim expression he always does when he is about to subject himself to a ride in an automobile, even one driven by as cautious a driver as I am. Like a dutiful chauffeur, I held the back door open for him, and he climbed inside with a grunt.

"The trip will take us about fifteen minutes at this time of night," I told him, "and I will make every effort to avoid potholes and pedestrians, although the latter, New Yorkers on foot, are a very unpredictable lot, dashing into traffic and risking life and limb. I promise I will do my very best to keep from hitting anyone."

"Archie, shut up!"

"Yes, sir. I was just making conversation." There was no more talk as I steered the Heron east and south, finally pulling up in front of the precinct station on Elizabeth Street, an unimpressive and narrow four-story structure jammed into a block with other buildings of similar height.

"This is the place," I told Wolfe. "Not much to look at, but then, police stations rarely are."

He made a snorting sound as I opened his door and gave him a hand as he stepped out onto the sidewalk. "Pfui, a disgusting edifice," he said as he glared up at the building. "Very well, we shall go in."

The husky desk sergeant looked up as we entered and blinked, perhaps reaction to Wolfe's dimensions. "Can I help you gentleman?"

"I believe Inspector Cramer is having a meeting here," I told him.

"Oh yes, I should have realized that's why you are here—it's Mr. Wolfe and Mr. Goodwin, right?" Before we could answer, he added, "Third door on the right."

Wolfe led the way down the bare hall, past two shabbily dressed men sitting on a bench and clearly waiting for someone. When we reached the door, I rapped on the pebbled glass and it swung open. The one who did the swinging was none other than Sergeant Purley Stebbins, Cramer's longtime sidekick and my longtime nemesis. We nodded to each other unsmiling, and Purley stepped aside so we could enter.

The room, typical of those you'll find in most police stations, was spartan, with bare walls, unwashed windows, and austere furnishings. The furnishings in this case were a long, gun-metal table and wooden chairs lined up on either side of it. The only people present, other than Stebbins, were Cramer and a uniformed officer.

"Okay, Wolfe, this is where we will be meeting," the inspector said curtly. "We'll bring the others in shortly, but I wanted you to meet Captain Kevin Ryan, who commands this precinct and is graciously letting us use this space tonight. Captain, this is Nero Wolfe and his assistant, Archie Goodwin, who are assisting us in a case."

"It is a pleasure to meet you, sir," the square-jawed, youthful cop said, holding out a hand. "I have heard and read a lot about you."

Wolfe, who is averse to shaking hands, had little choice in this case. After the ritual had been completed, including a shake between the captain and me, Wolfe thanked Ryan and looked around at the setup. The captain then left the room, leaving it to us.

"I know what's worrying you," Cramer said. "Purley, get that item from next door." Stebbins went into a connecting room and came out pushing a wheeled and padded desk chair with arms that looked like it could accommodate Wolfe.

"Put it right there," the inspector told his sergeant, who looked like he wanted to chew nails. Stebbins dislikes Wolfe as much as he does me, but he followed orders and slid the chair up to the table.

"Here is how this is going to work," Cramer told Wolfe. "You and I will sit on one side of the table, facing our 'guests,' and Purley will stand well behind them with his back against the wall. There are glasses of water for everyone at the table. Goodwin, you can take a chair and move it well back from the table. You are to be an onlooker here, and nothing more."

I could tell that Wolfe was seething, used as he was to controlling these sessions. But he remained silent, squeezing himself into the chair.

"All right, Purley," Cramer said, "it's time to bring the others in." Stebbins went out and was gone for several minutes. When he came back in, he held the door open and stepped aside. In trekked bar owner Liam McCready, Elmont building superintendent Erwin Bauer, the National Export pier boss, Doug Halliwell, and the closed-mouthed William Hartz, whose partner had dented my skull. None of them wore a smile.

"Gentlemen, thank you for coming," Cramer said. "Please take seats on that side of the table. As I have told each of you, the police department is investigating a series of events, perhaps related, more likely not, that have taken place in the Hell's Kitchen neighborhood recently. These include a murder, a fatal shooting in a bar—your bar, Mr. McCready—and two beatings. Now I have—"

"I still want to know what in God's name is going on!" interrupted Halliwell. "My pier has got nothing to do with whatever the hell has been happening in that neighborhood. And I want to know what these two guys are doing here." He pointed at Wolfe and me.

"If you let me finish, we can move on," Cramer said. "This gentleman is Nero Wolfe, a private detective, who has offered to help with our investigation. And the man over there is Archie Goodwin, a detective who works with Mr. Wolfe."

"A detective, hah!" Halliwell said. "He said he was a magazine writer when he interviewed me the other day. What kind of people are the police department using these days to help them? This Goodwin guy is either a phony writer or a phony private eye. Or maybe both."

"We can discuss Mr. Goodwin later," said a red-faced Cramer. "At this point, I am going to turn the proceedings over to Mr. Wolfe."

Wolfe readjusted himself in the chair and looked in turn at the four faces on the opposite side of the table. "I was drawn into the consecution of events listed by Mr. Cramer because of the vicious attack upon an employee of mine, Theodore Horstmann. And to take issue with the inspector, I believe all of the events he referred to are indeed related.

"Let us begin with Mr. Horstmann's beating: He had been one of a group of bridge players at your establishment, Mr. McCready. Others have told me he became suspicious of the behavior of some of the other patrons of the McCready establishment."

"I run a respectable place," the tavern owner snapped, starting to rise.

"Sit down!" Cramer said. "Everyone is going to get his say before this is over."

"The beating of an individual who happened to play cards in the back room of a tavern might not seem remarkable in and of itself," Wolfe continued. "But when a second member of that bridge foursome, Chester Miller, was found dead of a gunshot wound in the waters of the Hudson off Hell's Kitchen, that occurrence taxed the credulity of even the most naïve and trusting individual. And lest there be any suggestion of a coincidence, it should be noted that, like Theodore Horstmann, the late Mr. Miller also harbored suspicions as to the activities of some of the habitués of the bar, be they longshoremen or others."

"My men are not the only dockworkers who go to McCready's," Halliwell said heatedly. "I don't know why you should single them out. Hell, I don't even know why I'm here at all!"

"Your invitation will become clear in the course of the evening," Wolfe said. "If I were you, I would not be in a hurry to hear an explanation of your presence."

"I have to agree with Doug Halliwell in wondering why I've been asked to come," Liam McCready put in. "I'm afraid I did not get a very good explanation from the inspector."

Cramer said, "I would suggest that both of you, and the others as well"—he gestured toward Bauer and Hartz—"be patient and let Mr. Wolfe proceed. I know from experience that he is not a man to be rushed."

"So," Wolfe continued, "we have two card players from the public house in Tenth Avenue who appeared to be singled out for violence. But why? It would appear, Mr. McCready, that being a customer in your establishment could be detrimental to one's health."

"Hold on there," the tavern keeper said. "They weren't what you would call 'customers,' I just let them use the space so they could enjoy their card games."

"But did they not purchase drinks from your establishment?" Wolfe asked.

"Well yes . . . but . . ."

"By any definition I am familiar with, that act would make those gentlemen customers of yours, would it not?"

"Well, all right, sort of," McCready said, his tone subdued. "I'm frightfully sorry for what happened to them."

"I am sure you are. Can you offer any explanation as to why they were singled out and targeted?"

"My bar has always been a peaceful spot, where people can come to socialize and relax and play pool."

"And play cards?"

"Yes, and play cards, as well."

"But your bar isn't always peaceful, is it, sir?" Wolfe went on. "What about the man you shot recently?"

McCready bristled. "I have told the police all about that."

Wolfe turned to Cramer with a questioning expression. "We're still continuing our investigation, but it appears that Mr. McCready acted in self-defense," the inspector said.

"Was the man you shot, named Emil Krueger, a regular customer of yours?" Wolfe asked.

"I wouldn't call him a regular, but he did come in on occasion for a beer or two."

"I realize you already have related to the police the series of events that night, but if you will indulge me, I would like to hear your description of the incident."

McCready looked at Cramer, hoping for support, but he was to be disappointed. The inspector curtly nodded for him to continue.

"I often stay in my small office in the back after the bar has closed. It seems there is always some paperwork to go over, and I also review the day's receipts."

"You do not take money to an overnight depository?"

"I prefer my financial dealings to be face-to-face," McCready said. "You can call it old-fashioned, but that was always the way people I knew did business back in Ireland."

"While in your office, you told the police you heard noises out in the public area of your establishment, and you went to investigate."

"That is correct, as I have said Lord knows how many times now."

"And you had a gun with you?"

"Yes, I keep a revolver in the office, just because—well, you never know."

"Please continue."

"It was dark there, of course, but just enough light was coming through the front window from the street that I could see a silhouetted figure, and he was holding a gun."

"Did you recognize him?"

"No, not at all."

"And what did he say?"

"He didn't say anything, he just pointed a gun at me like he was going to use it, and I fired my own, just once."

"But once was enough, wasn't it?" Wolfe said.

"I was sure that he was going to shoot me!" McCready shouted.

"Did you have reason to fear Mr. Krueger?"

"I didn't even know it was him when I shot. I didn't know who it was in the dark."

"Were you in Ireland when the war broke out?"

"No, I came here in the late 1930s. My uncle, who had run the bar before me, had died, and I was fortunate enough to assume the ownership."

"Did you see service during the war?"

"No, I was not yet an American citizen."

"But that should not have mattered," Wolfe said. "The Second War Powers Act in 1942 exempted noncitizens who joined the armed forces from naturalization requirements. And you certainly were of an age to serve."

"Well, I . . . felt that I needed to be here to run the family business that was entrusted to me," McCready said.

"If you had still been in Ireland during the war, would you have served in the British forces?"

"Perhaps you do not understand, Mr. Wolfe, that Ireland—at least the Free State, not Ulster—remained neutral during the war. How could I have served?"

"Oh, but I do understand, sir. I also am aware that thousands of Irish citizens joined the British military. Those who deserted the Irish army to join with their neighbors were both shamed and shunned after the war."

"And well they should have been!" McCready said heatedly. "They had no business fighting with the English."

"I gather you do not like the English."

"I do not, and why should I, the way they have treated Ireland over the centuries?"

"So, in dealing with what you might have seen as two evils, would you have preferred to see Germany victorious, rather than the Allies?"

"Are you trying to trick me?"

"Trick you?" Wolfe said, his face registering innocence. "Why would I do that, Mr. McCready? I am simply trying to determine where your loyalties lay in that war. As an American now, I would have thought you would prefer to see the Allies prevail."

"You clearly are not familiar with the misery the Irish have endured at the hands of those cursed people in London."

"I am familiar with it, although not in a personal way. And I do possess some familiarity with the behavior of the Axis during the war, as I have relatives in Eastern Europe who have experienced that behavior, to their detriment."

Wolfe turned his attention to the Elmont super. "You, sir, appear to have had the opportunity to meet many recent arrivals from Europe. How have you found their physical condition and their state of mind?"

Erwin Bauer jerked upright as one awakened from a stupor. "What . . . do you mean?" he said, like a student who hadn't been listening to his teacher and seemed startled by the question.

"I have been made aware that many of the residents of your building are recent immigrants from Europe, is that not so?" Wolfe posed.

Bauer swallowed hard. "Yes, yes, it is."

"How are these people drawn to the Elmont?"

Now Bauer was plenty alert all right, but jumpy as well. "They must have heard about it from others who have come. It is a good place to live."

"Would you say, Mr. Bauer, that many, or even most, of these people residing in the Elmont are displaced persons?"

He nodded.

"Do they possess the proper identification that entitles them to be in this country?"

I almost felt sorry for the skinny man in his ill-fitting clothes, but not quite. He looked at Halliwell on his left and McCready on his right as if expecting help in answering. Neither of them stirred.

"It really is not my job to check the identification of tenants," Bauer said.

"Whose job is it, sir?"

"That would be the company that manages the building," Bauer replied as beads of perspiration sprouted on his freckled forehead and he gulped water from his glass.

"Do they indeed do some checking?"

"I don't know what has been done by them before people who are seeking rooms come to me."

"What is the name of the company that manages the Elmont?" Wolfe demanded.

"Uh . . . Merritt and Day Properties, over in . . . Jersey City," the super said. Wolfe turned to me with a beckoning look. I got up and bent down next to him as he whispered instructions in my ear. I nodded, left the room, and sought a pay phone.

When I returned after no more than ten minutes, Wolfe was addressing Douglas Halliwell. "... and do you carry passengers on your ship, sir?"

"No, we are strictly a freight operation."

"It has been reported that persons have been seen debarking from your ships who do not appear to resemble either crew members or longshoremen."

"Reported by who?" Halliwell demanded.

"That is immaterial, sir."

"Yeah? Well, I'd like someone try proving that we're carrying passengers."

Wolfe ignored the remark, turning to me with a questioning expression. I got up and handed him a note I had written after my phone call. I received a glare from Cramer, as if to remind me that tonight I was an onlooker and nothing more. I glared back.

CHAPTER 34

After reading what I had handed him, Wolfe gulped his glass of water, made a face, and turned his attention back to the Elmont building superintendent. "Mr. Bauer, are you acquainted with Wesley Merritt, of Merritt and Day Properties?"

"Yes, sir," he said.

"Would you consider him to be a trustworthy individual?"

Erwin Bauer tensed. "Uh . . . yes, of course he is."

"Mr. Merritt appears to be not only trustworthy, but hard-working as well. He was still in his office at this late hour when my associate, Mr. Goodwin, talked to him by telephone a few minutes ago. He asked Mr. Merritt whose responsibility it is to verify the identification papers of persons who seek rooms in the Elmont. Would you like to hear his response?"

Bauer went from tensing to squirming. "I . . ."

When nothing more came from the super's lips, Wolfe read my handwriting aloud. "As we trust him implicitly, we leave it to Erwin Bauer to evaluate the people who want to live in the Elmont. We have told him, of course, that if he has any question at all about a request from a potential lodger, he should talk either to me or to my partner, Lloyd Day. I can't think of a single incident where he has felt the need to call us about such a request. Has someone complained about Erwin?"

Wolfe set the paper down on the table and addressed Bauer. "Mr. Goodwin told Mr. Merritt that he knew of no complaints about you, if that sets your mind at ease. I have a complaint, however, as seems patently obvious. You are a fabricator—or do you prefer liar? You apparently are the sole gatekeeper at the Elmont, the one individual who decides on the makeup of the building. Or do you have assistance in the selection process?"

Both McCready and Halliwell were looking daggers at the little man, who seemed to be shrinking in his chair. "Come, come, sir," Wolfe said to Bauer. "You have been caught out. I am confident that when—and it now is only a matter of time—the authorities take a close look at the backgrounds of the Elmont residents, you will be called to account as the individual who admitted them. The question I pose to you: Will you run yourself through with a sword and, to use a phrase Mr. Goodwin likes, 'take the fall,' or will you implicate others to lessen your own punishment? The choice becomes yours."

Bauer seemed to be in a daze. He looked down and kept shaking his head. It was obvious to me that the man was nearing a breaking point. For a half-minute, although it seemed longer, no one in the room said a word.

Finally, Bauer broke the silence, speaking hesitantly and hoarsely. The super turned toward Halliwell and said, "He brings people to me and tells me to give them apartments." Halliwell grimaced and started to rise, but one of Purley Stebbins's large hands gripped his shoulder and pushed him back down.

"How would you describe the individuals Mr. Halliwell presents to you?" Wolfe asked.

"They are mostly foreign men."

"From what countries, Mr. Bauer?"

"They seem to be German, and maybe Austrian or Dutch, I cannot tell."

"Did you ask to see any identification?"

"No, I was told that was not necessary."

"Told by whom?"

"Mr. Halliwell."

Wolfe addressed the longshoreman. "Would you like to explain your actions?"

"I don't have any idea what he's talking about," Halliwell said, passing a hand over his crew cut. "I barely know the man."

Wolfe scowled. "Let us now turn to this gentleman," he said, directing his attention to William Hartz, who had been ignored up to now. "Sir, you have been charged with assault and the attempted murder of my colleague Mr. Goodwin. Do you have anything to say?"

Hartz, who was at least six feet tall but looked like he had shrunk within his prison garb, shook his head.

"We're told that he has been eating very little," Cramer put in.

"I understand you have been informed that you are entitled to legal counsel but as yet have refused it. Is that correct?" Wolfe asked. Hartz said nothing.

"Very well. Perhaps you feel the silent treatment and a hunger strike are your best approaches to your situation. I can assure you they will not help. If you think you are aiding anyone in this room by your silence, you are badly mistaken. If anything, your cause will be harmed by your actions."

When Hartz remained silent, Wolfe sighed. "You were shot in the leg after the assault upon Mr. Goodwin here. Has your wound healed?"

Hartz actually nodded. "Well, that is something," Wolfe said. "You had an accomplice in that attack, and he is the one who delivered the blow to my associate, not you. Yet you are the one who is in jail. That seems hardly fair to you, does it?"

The man blinked and pursed his lips. I could see that Wolfe was getting to Hartz, and he was not about to let up. "You may think you are being a loyal friend by protecting your colleague, and whomever else was directing your actions, Mr. Hartz. But I assure you that your loyalty will not be returned or rewarded in any way whatever. If you remain silent, your punishment will be greater than if you cooperate with the police and tell them who has been giving you orders. Those people very likely are laughing at you right now."

"I do not . . . like . . . being laughed at," Hartz said in heavily accented English.

"Nor should you," Wolfe replied as Cramer and Stebbins both showed surprise at words coming out of this clam. "Who directed you to attack Mr. Goodwin?"

Hartz stiffened, and I figured, here we go again, the guy is going to get lockjaw, to use Cramer's word. But damned if he didn't turn and point a finger at Liam McCready, who recoiled as if hit with a cattle prod. "What in the name of the Lord are you talking about!" the barkeep shouted at Hartz.

"He is not talking, merely pointing, Mr. McCready," Wolfe said. "But it is a meaningful gesture. Perhaps you would care to respond."

"Not to this man I wouldn't. I don't even know him."

"Now you can see, Mr. Hartz, how Jesus of Nazareth must have felt in that fateful garden when his friend Peter denied any knowledge of their relationship."

"I know that story from the Bible," Hartz said, shaking his head and looking sadly at McCready, who would not return his glance.

"Some time ago, Inspector Cramer, I mentioned the term 'ratline,' which you were unfamiliar with. This is not surprising, as the word has not been in general use for long. What we have here is a ratline, and I—"

"Get to the point, Wolfe!"

"That is where I am headed. A few years ago, at a speech in Missouri, Winston Churchill coined the phrase, 'Iron Curtain,' to describe the way the Soviet Union had in effect taken over many countries in Eastern Europe after the war. At the risk of aping Mr. Churchill, I am going to suggest that what we have here is an 'Iron Triangle,' a local system of smuggling a certain category of individuals into the United States."

"Do mean Communists?" Cramer asked in a shocked tone.

"No, Nazis," Wolfe said. "That is what this business has been all about." The room got very quiet, as if no one wanted to say a word. Having achieved the effect that he sought, Wolfe went on.

"Ratlines are systems by which Nazis of all ranks have been smuggled out of Germany since the end of the war to countries around the world. Many of the most high-ranking members of Hitler's National Socialist Party fled to South America, primarily Brazil and Argentina, as has been widely reported. Far less publicity has been given to other locations where Nazis have been able to find refuge, including Peru, Uruguay, Bolivia, Guatemala, Mexico, and, yes, the United States."

"What about this so-called Iron Triangle of yours?' Cramer demanded of Wolfe.

"Thank you for getting us back to the subject at hand, Inspector. The deeper I delved into this perplexity, the more obvious it became that there were several moving parts. To smuggle Nazis into this country took a number of individuals working in concert. Three of them are in this room."

"Now wait a minute!" Liam McCready said, "I want to protest this—"

"No, *you* wait a minute," Cramer cut in. "Mr. Wolfe has the floor, and that will be the case until I say otherwise."

"Thank you, Inspector. Our triangle, as I choose to describe it, begins with Douglas Halliwell, or more accurately, with a colleague of his at National Export Lines in Germany. These men, working together, have moved Nazis across the Atlantic to New York via the shipping company's freighters.

"Along with his German partner, Mr. Halliwell, an avowed admirer of the National Socialist German Workers Party, i.e., the Nazis, charged these men to transport them to our shores. I leave it to others to determine the rates that got extracted from these 'passengers.'

"Once ashore in New York, the men—and most if not all of the Nazi arrivals are male—are directed by Mr. Halliwell to the Elmont establishment on Tenth Avenue, where they are greeted by our Mr. Bauer here. How did he become the second leg in our triangle? Perhaps he can edify us."

Bauer stared at his lap, and after several seconds, he spoke without looking up. "I am an American citizen. I came here twenty years ago, even before Hitler became powerful, because I did not like it in Germany. My parents stayed, and they both died of diseases before the war. My brother also chose to stay. According to what Halliwell has told me, Dieter—that's my brother—was being investigated by the American forces now in Germany because he was accused of being a Nazi."

"Had you known that before?" Wolfe asked.

"No, but I was not surprised. Dieter had always liked the military life, and the uniforms. If Dieter stayed in Germany, he probably would have been executed, Halliwell told me, but he felt he could get him over here without the Americans knowing it."

"On a National Export ship?" Wolfe posed.

Bauer finally looked up, nodding. "Yes, but there was a price. I had to agree to shelter at the Elmont others who came over on those ships of Halliwell's."

"Which you did?"

Bauer nodded again. "I have never liked the Nazis or what they stand for, but I also love Dieter, so I agreed."

"I gather there were empty apartments at the Elmont."

"Yes, the building had not really been so popular in recent times, and when these . . . Nazis began filling it, Mr. Merritt and Mr. Day were very pleased."

"Did they know many of their new tenants were Nazis?" Wolfe asked.

"Well . . . no, I saw no reason to tell them."

"Has your brother been staying at the Elmont?"

"No, he has gone to some other part of the city. He would not tell me where, and I don't know the address. We only met for a short time when he arrived here."

"How did these men have the ability to pay the rent at the Elmont?"

"They could not even come across the ocean unless they had several hundred American dollars. I do not know the exact figure, and my brother would not tell me. He also did not tell me how he got the money."

"I assume some of it, and that of the other passengers as well, went to Mr. Halliwell and his friend in Germany at the shipping company," Wolfe said.

"I do not know that," Bauer said. "What I do know is that all of these men had enough money to pay for at least their first two months' rent."

"How much of that money did you keep for yourself?"

"None of it!" Bauer snapped, sounding offended. "I did not need it. Merritt and Day pay me a fair salary."

Wolfe glared at his empty water glass and sighed. "Now let us turn our attention to Mr. McCready and his public house."

CHAPTER 35

The tavern owner shifted uneasily in his chair as Wolfe considered him through lidded eyes. "So now we come to the final leg of our triangle," he said. "Mr. McCready, a number of the newer residents of the Elmont have been seen in your establishment."

"So what?" McCready said. "We are right across the street, so it is an obvious place to go. Are you suggesting that it is illegal to have a drink?"

"By no means. It has been almost twenty years since the Volstead Act was repealed. I would like to return to your relationship with Emil Krueger, who you shot dead in your establishment."

"In self-defense!"

"Perhaps," Wolfe said, shifting his attention to William Hartz. "Were you acquainted with Mr. Krueger?"

The man in prison garb tensed. "Answer the question!" Cramer prodded.

"Yes . . . I knew him, but only from having seen him in the tavern."

"I am going to suggest you knew him very well," Wolfe said. "He was the other man with you in the attack on Mr. Goodwin, wasn't he?"

Hartz drank from his water glass, as if hoping to postpone his response. When he set the glass down, he was met with Wolfe's steady, unrelenting gaze.

"I don't want to tell you again to answer Mr. Wolfe," Cramer urged.

"Emil was with me, yes. He . . . was the one who hit Mr. Goodwin."

"And this was not the only time the pair of you attacked people, was it?" Wolfe asked.

Hartz looked at Cramer, as if he was about to feel the inspector's anger yet again. "No, it was not," he said, his accented voice just above a whisper.

"Tell us about these attacks, Mr. Hartz."

"Two were of men who played cards at Mr. McCready's tavern."

"What happened to them?"

"One, a heavy man, was . . . shot dead by Krueger."

"What became of the body?"

"We . . . put it in the river."

"And the other one?"

"He was struck on the head by . . . me on a street, but a car came along. We ran away and left him."

"So, you do not know what happened to him?" Hartz shook his head.

"Why did you attack these men—and Mr. Goodwin?"

"I was ordered to."

"By whom?" Wolfe demanded.

"Them," Hartz said, looking first at Halliwell and then at McCready, neither of whom stirred.

"Why would these two want those individuals harmed?"

"We were told they . . . they were suspicious and dangerous."

"Are you going to believe this guy?" Halliwell barked. "He's just trying to save his own skin. He doesn't know what he's talking about."

"Were you paid for following these orders?" Cramer put in, ignoring Halliwell's outburst.

"We were supposed to be given money by Mr. McCready, and Emil went to see him."

"What was the result of that visit?" Wolfe asked.

Hartz sighed. "Emil, he . . . he got shot."

"This man is a goddamn liar!" McCready shouted. "Doug Halliwell is right; he doesn't know what he's talking about. Krueger came to the bar that night to rob me, it is as simple as that."

"Mr. Krueger can hardly dispute your version of that encounter," Wolfe said. "If that encounter came after closing hours, how did he get inside the establishment? I assume you lock the doors at two a.m."

"He must have been hiding in one of the bathrooms," McCready said.

"Are those areas not checked when you close up?"

"I must have forgotten that night," the tavern keeper answered, swallowing hard.

"That night of all nights," Wolfe observed. "Convenient."

"Now wait a minute, you are not going to pin a murder on me; I acted in self-defense," McCready said.

"But you do admit a bullet from your weapon killed Mr. Krueger," Wolfe said.

"The police have heard my story and have chosen to believe

it, as well they should. Who are they going to believe, me or some DP?"

Wolfe turned to Cramer. "When the police arrived at the tavern and found Mr. Krueger's body, was a weapon found near it?"

"Yes, and with his fingerprints on it. One chamber in the revolver was empty, suggesting it well might have been the gun that killed Miller."

"As far as could be determined, did that revolver on the floor belong to the dead man?"

"We can't know that for sure, as it was not licensed," the inspector said. "A search of Krueger's room at the Elmont failed to discover any weapon, so we are left to assume that the gun found next to the dead man's body was one he had carried into the tavern."

"Let me propose this scenario," Wolfe said. "Krueger asked for a meeting with Mr. McCready to discuss a payment from him for the murder of Chester Miller and the beatings of two other individuals, including Mr. Goodwin.

"The tavern keeper agreed to a meeting after closing time at the bar. In the ensuing conversation, Krueger demanded payment and likely physically threatened McCready, who then shot the displaced person."

"This is absolute tripe!" McCready yelled. "Why would I want to have anything to do with a Nazi like Krueger? I told you I barely knew him."

"So you say. We have already established your dislike for the British," Wolfe said. "As an Irishman, you have good reason for that dislike, given the ill-treatment your native country endured for centuries at the hands of its neighboring island. However, Irish animus toward Britain during and since the war has come with a by-product: support for Germany and, as a corollary, sympathy for the Nazis. I want to make it clear that by no means do all Irish share this feeling. Many thousands of them supported the Allied cause and fought with valor in the British forces during the war."

I expected Liam McCready to react to Wolfe's statement, but he sat on his hands and said nothing.

"What we have here," Wolfe went on, "is one of several operations by which uncounted numbers of Nazis have anonymously arrived on our shores. As I said earlier, many of the higher-profile members of that odious movement landed in South America. But others, among them concentration camp guards and other staff, military officers, and foot soldiers, have managed to meld into the populace in this country and in this city."

"What would I have to gain by protecting these people?" McCready argued, jabbing a thump at his chest.

"From what I have been told, many of these recent arrivals have become patrons of your establishment," Wolfe said, "which of course brings you added revenue. Also, you—and Mr. Halliwell—no doubt extort funds from these recent arrivals in return for your promises of secrecy."

"You can't prove that!" Halliwell snapped.

"I will leave it for others to do the verifying," Wolfe replied. "What I have provided is an outline."

"Purley, escort these four to the next room," Cramer ordered.

"Wait a minute," Halliwell said, "just what is going on here?"

"I will be with all of you shortly," the inspector said as the quartet rose and were ushered out by the Purley Stebbins. When they had gone, Cramer turned to Wolfe. "The evidence against this bunch seems pretty sparse to me."

"As I said, you now have an outline, and you have an army to investigate the culpability of each of those individuals, where I have only a handful of agents."

"What's in this for you, Wolfe?"

"The satisfaction that I have identified those who assaulted Theodore Horstmann."

"Huh! Do you have a client?"

"Not that it is any business of yours, but I do, sir."

Cramer shrugged. "All right, so be it. Needless to say, we are going to give these bastards a real going over—without any physical violence, of course."

"Of course."

I could tell the inspector had been appalled at what was revealed, or at least suggested, during the meeting. Here was a cop who had observed a lot of evil in his decades on the force, but this may have topped everything else he had seen. And his hatred of the Axis forces was no doubt deepened by his son's military service in Australia during the war.

CHAPTER 36

Inspector Cramer and his men must have done a good job in their "going over" of the four men, because any original denials from them soon turned to admissions, and each of the quartet is in the process of facing trial, along with three of Halliwell's crew members on the National Export docks who had taken an active role in the smuggling operation. In addition, according to the *Gazette* reporting, at least a score of former Nazis, many of them residents of the Elmont, has been rounded up.

To back up slightly, after we got back to the brownstone from the Lower East Side precinct that night, I telephoned Lon Cohen at the *Gazette* and gave him a general outline of what had transpired, along with a suggestion that he talk to Cramer. I also told him that Wolfe's name was not to appear in any articles involving what had transpired.

Lon and the *Gazette* jumped all over the story, beating the competition from the start. The paper's first headline in what was to be a continuing series read: RING THAT SMUGGLED NAZIS INTO N.Y. IS SMASHED!

After all the hullabaloo, life began returning to normal in the brownstone, including one particularly positive note: Theodore Horstmann had at last emerged from his coma, and, according to Doc Vollmer, his mental functions appeared to be undiminished. For the first several weeks after his release from the hospital, he stayed with his sister over in New Jersey, but it was clear that he was itching to get back to the orchids. Speaking of Frieda, she tried to get Wolfe to accept more money from her for his efforts, but he flatly refused, saying simply, "I have accomplished what I set out to do."

Theodore's recovery was gradual and took many months. He started coming across the Hudson one day a week, and then two, being that Vollmer had prescribed for him a gradual reentry into his former work schedule.

Once he had fully recovered, Theodore related to us, and to Inspector Cramer, his memory of the beating he took. With him grumbling all the way, I drove Theodore to Rikers Island where, through a one-way glass, he identified William Hartz as one of the two men who had attacked him as he walked that fateful night a few blocks from the Elmont. He also viewed a death photograph of Emil Krueger and said that he "looked like" the other man in the attack, although he could not be positive.

As for Carl Willis, who had filled in as Wolfe's orchid nurse, he was happy enough to begin relinquishing his temporary role. The two had managed to tolerate each other, although the relationship was never smooth and certainly far from amiable. Wolfe considered the new man to be marginally knowledgeable about the orchidaceous world. Willis, in turn, felt that his overseer was a martinet who criticized his every move. I know this, because I heard his complaints almost every time he came downstairs to give me the orchid germination material to enter into the files.

It was a sure thing that the "team" of Wolfe and Willis would soon be dissolved, and that Theodore would eventually be returning to the plant rooms on the top floor of the brownstone on a full-time basis. Where he would live was yet to be determined, but it definitely would not be in a certain five-story building on Tenth Avenue in the heart of Manhattan's Hell's Kitchen.

AUTHOR'S NOTE

The preceding work is fiction, but the saga of Nazis infiltrating the United States after World War II is far from fictional. An instructive volume in the writing of this story is *The Nazis Next Door: How America Became a Safe Haven for Hitler's Men* by Eric Lichtblau (Houghton Mifflin Harcourt; Boston; New York, 2014). In his book, two-time Pulitzer Prize–winning newspaperman Lichtblau shows how Nazis, many of them using forged identification, came to the United States and managed to blend into the society, in numerous cases reinventing themselves and building new lives and careers, not just in New York, but elsewhere as well. The book makes chilling reading.

One striking example is that of a German-born woman who during the immediate postwar years lived in anonymity as a housewife in Queens, married to an American construction worker. It was later discovered that she was a guard at a Nazi concentration camp who regularly beat women prisoners and killed several of them. She was returned to Germany, tried, and imprisoned for life. She was released for health reasons three years before her death in 1999.

In addition to the Lichtblau work, I have relied on several other sources, each of which has been helpful in increasing my knowledge and appreciation of the Nero Wolfe corpus, which Rex Stout developed over more than four decades. These are: *Nero Wolfe of West Thirty-Fifth Street: The Life and Times of America's Largest Private Detective* by William Baring-Gould (Viking Press, New York, 1968); *The Nero Wolfe Cookbook* by Rex Stout and the Editors of Viking Press (Viking Press, New York, 1973); *The Brownstone House of Nero Wolfe* by Ken Darby as told by Archie Goodwin (Little, Brown & Co. Boston, Toronto, 1983); and *Rex Stout: A Biography* by John McAleer (Little, Brown & Co., Boston, 1977). The McAleer book won an Edgar Award in the biography category from the Mystery Writers of America.

I give my heartfelt gratitude to Rex Stout's daughter, Rebecca Stout Bradbury. Rebecca has been a continuing source of support and encouragement in my continuation of her father's wonderfully developed characters and settings.

My thanks and my appreciation also go to my agent, Martha Kaplan, to Otto Penzler and Charles Perry of Mysterious Press, and to the strong team at Open Road Integrated Media.

And a tip of the hat to my long-time friend and encourager Max Allan Collins, an award-winning mystery author and screenwriter. Max suggested to me that I write a Nero Wolfe story in which Theodore Horstmann would play a larger part than is usually the case. This I have done, although Mr. Horstmann would hardly have appreciated the role to which he was consigned in this narrative.

AUTHOR'S NOTE

As a final and most important note, both my love and my boundless thanks go to Janet, my wife and guiding star of more than fifty-five years, who continues to be my greatest source of inspiration. Without her, I would be incomplete and rudderless.

ABOUT THE AUTHOR

Robert Goldsborough is an American author best known for continuing Rex Stout's famous Nero Wolfe series. Born in Chicago, he attended Northwestern University and upon graduation went to work for the Associated Press, beginning a lifelong career in journalism that would include long periods at the *Chicago Tribune* and *Advertising Age*. While at the *Tribune*, Goldsborough began writing mysteries in the voice of Rex Stout, the creator of iconic sleuths Nero Wolfe and Archie Goodwin. Goldsborough's first novel starring Wolfe, *Murder in E Minor* (1986), was met with acclaim from both critics and devoted fans, winning a Nero Award from the Wolfe Pack. *Trouble at the Brownstone* is the sixteenth book in the series.

THE NERO WOLFE MYSTERIES

FROM MYSTERIOUSPRESS.COM
AND OPEN ROAD MEDIA

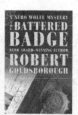

MYSTERIOUSPRESS.COM

Otto Penzler, owner of the Mysterious Bookshop in Manhattan, founded the Mysterious Press in 1975. Penzler quickly became known for his outstanding selection of mystery, crime, and suspense books, both from his imprint and in his store. The imprint was devoted to printing the best books in these genres, using fine paper and top dust-jacket artists, as well as offering many limited, signed editions.

Now the Mysterious Press has gone digital, publishing ebooks through **MysteriousPress.com**.

MysteriousPress.com offers readers essential noir and suspense fiction, hard-boiled crime novels, and the latest thrillers from both debut authors and mystery masters. Discover classics and new voices, all from one legendary source.

FIND OUT MORE AT
WWW.MYSTERIOUSPRESS.COM

FOLLOW US:
@emysteries and Facebook.com/MysteriousPressCom

MysteriousPress.com is one of a select group of publishing partners of Open Road Integrated Media, Inc.

THe MYSTeRIOUS BOOKSHOP, founded in 1979, is located in Manhattan's Tribeca neighborhood. It is the oldest and largest mystery-specialty bookstore in America.

The shop stocks the finest selection of new mystery hardcovers, paperbacks, and periodicals. It also features a superb collection of signed modern first editions, rare and collectable works, and Sherlock Holmes titles. The bookshop issues a free monthly newsletter highlighting its book clubs, new releases, events, and recently acquired books.

58 Warren Street
info@mysteriousbookshop.com
(212) 587-1011
Monday through Saturday
11:00 a.m. to 7:00 p.m.

FIND OUT MORE AT:

www.mysteriousbookshop.com

FOLLOW US:

@TheMysterious and Facebook.com/MysteriousBookshop

INTEGRATED MEDIA